WALKER DEFENSE

BERNADETTE MARIE

5 Prince Publishing

Published by 5 PRINCE PUBLISHING & BOOKS, LLC

PO Box 865, Arvada, CO 80001

www.5PrinceBooks.com

ISBN digital: 978-1-63112-237-8

ISBN print: 978-1-63112-238-5

Cover Credit: Bernadette Soehner

❀ Created with Vellum

Stan,
Thank you for always having my back and coming to my defense when needed.

I love you!

ACKNOWLEDGMENTS

To my men: I will always defend you because I love you so much!

To Mom and Sissy: Thank you for being my counsel when I need it.

To Cate: Thank you for being you, being there, and being awesome!

To my AWESOME readers: Thank you for loving the Walker family and wanting to read their stories.

OTHER TITLES BY

WALKER DEFENSE

On a warm day, in the garden of Glenda Walker, laughter and applause enveloped all the guests at the wedding of Ben and Nichole.

Ella wiped the tears from her cheeks with a handkerchief as she watched Ben, Nichole, and *their* three children welcome their congratulations from Ben's brothers.

She envied the relationship the Walker family had with one another. Five boys, each one so different and strong-willed, yet compassionate and emotional when it mattered. She'd seen them go at it a time or two. Fists and words could be flung around, blood might be drawn, but they always had each other's back.

Ella came from a good family. Her mother and father had been married thirty years at Christmas, and her sister was married happily with a growing family, but they didn't have the same bond the Walkers had. They no longer lived in the same town or the same state. They were content with emails and phone calls to stay connected.

The Walkers—they worked together, ate together, and ran with the same people. They were present in each other's lives.

Perhaps that made her a little weepy, and today wasn't a day to sob over her own life. It was a day to celebrate Ben and Nichole, and their children.

Ella had spent a lot of time with Nichole over the past nine months as they prosecuted the woman who had stolen Nichole's identity and attacked Ben. As far as Ella was concerned, Nichole and her family would never have to worry about her again, but there would be lingering after-effects from fraud for a while.

Once that case had been mostly handled, and the woman was convicted and put in jail, Ben had approached her about adopting Nichole's kids. For the adoption to take place, their father had to give up rights to his children. Considering he was in jail on embezzlement charges, he wasn't too worried about keeping his parental rights. Ella was sickened by how quickly he signed them away.

She watched as Ben and Nichole, and their little family walked down the aisle headed back toward the house. They stopped when they came to her, and both hugged her.

"Thank you for everything," Nichole whispered in her ear.

"My pleasure," she said as the family moved on, followed by their attendants.

Swiping a thumb over her cheek, she wiped away a stray tear as Gerald Walker followed his brother down the aisle. His eyes automatically darted to her, and a nervous grin curled up the corner of his mouth before he quickly looked away.

Ella couldn't blame him for being nervous around her. She'd broken his heart, crushed his plans, belittled him in front of his family. It had been years ago, but the pain remained. Angry with herself, she felt the heat rise in her cheeks. She was lucky even to be welcomed into their home, she thought.

But as Glenda Walker passed by her, she reached out her hand and gave Ella's a squeeze accompanied by a friendly smile. Perhaps she was too hard on herself. The Walkers hadn't pushed her out of their lives. She'd stepped back away from them out of respect. However, when they'd needed her expertise, they'd called on her. For that, she'd been grateful. It was the least she could do for a family that had once embraced her as one of their own.

The wedding reception would follow at Lydia Morgan's reception hall in town. With the venue forty-five minutes away, she wondered if they'd notice if she didn't attend.

As the guests began to stroll out of the garden, she caught the eye of Nichole who waved with a smile, again obviously grateful to have her there. Well, maybe they'd notice.

She was heading back into town anyway. She might as well stop by the reception, have some food, and perhaps a glass of champagne. Wedding cake was always a good reason to attend a reception… that and Susan Walker's catering.

It would be worth the slight discomfort to celebrate the marriage of Ben Walker.

As Ella started her BMW, which she'd parked down the road, she heard her name called from behind her. When she turned, she saw Gerald hurrying toward her.

"Hey, might sound crazy, but can I get a ride into town with you? Cars are full of gifts and wedding party. I seem to be the odd man out," he said as he reached her.

She knew she was staring, and for the first time in her life seemed to be out of words.

"If you have other plans I can…"

"No, no," she stammered. "I can give you a ride. No problem."

Her heart hitched when he smiled that smile she'd seen so many times years ago. She'd been sure she'd never see it again aimed in her direction, but here it was.

Unsure of what to say next, Ella opened her car door and climbed in. When Gerald didn't open his door right away, she looked toward it to see him standing there motioning to unlock it.

"I'm sorry," she said as he climbed in. "I'm a little nervous being around you and your family today."

"You've been around my family for nearly nine months

working with Nichole on her case. What's making you nervous now?"

She started the engine, and the car roared to life. "I've spent that time with Nichole, not so much with Ben, or you, or the rest of your family. Gerald, I know how they all feel about me. I know what I did, and I know…"

"You don't know anything," he argued with a bite in his voice. "I get every right to be mad at you for the rest of my life."

"Yes, you do," she agreed.

"But you know my family damn well enough to know that angry or not, they wouldn't mistreat you."

As she put the car in drive and began to follow the other cars down the dirt road to town, she resigned to the pity party she'd been having. Gerald was right. His family, including him, would never treat her poorly for her decisions.

"I'm sorry for all of that. I'm just nervous."

"I get it. I'm nervous too, but I don't want to be. We were friends for years so why not start as friends now?"

Ella bit down on her glossed lip. "You're sure you want to be my friend?"

"Are you getting resettled in town and trying to build your career?"

"Yes."

"Have you been gone long enough that some things have changed?"

"Yes."

"Are you divorced and trying to work through that in your head and your heart?"

That stung she thought, but she answered honestly. "Yes."

"Then it sounds like you could use a friend, so why not me? And you don't have to worry. I don't get to town too often, so I won't be one of those 'drop by and stand on your porch' kind of friends. You don't have to open up to me and confess all your sins or desires. You don't have to defend any decision you've ever made. We can consider ourselves simply friends."

As she paced her vehicle behind the car in front of her to give herself visibility from the dust kicking up, she considered his offer. She missed Gerald Walker in every way, but mostly as her friend. That had been an enormous loss when she'd turned down his marriage proposal.

"I'd like to be friends," she admitted. "I had considered not going to the reception. I thought I might feel out of place."

"That would be a shame if you missed it."

"It seems as though I've missed my share of Walker weddings in the past few years. I can't say I saw that coming," she humored as he fidgeted with the radio, a habit he'd always had when he'd get into her car.

"I don't think any of them thought they'd all be getting married. And now there are kids, too. Who'd have thought?"

Well, they had, she considered. They'd talked about marriage. They'd made plans. Oh, they were stupid and young and foolish, but they'd thought about it. And until the moment he'd asked her to marry him, she'd been right there with him making those plans. But she got spooked, and she'd landed in the arms of his best friend. Ex-best friend, she noted.

"They all seem very happy."

"They are. I guess there is someone for everyone," he offered, as he found a song he liked, for the time being, and sat back in his seat. "So what about you? Are you dating anyone?"

Ella swallowed the lump in her throat. This drive was long enough without talking about dating with her ex.

"No. Not very interested in dating right now. My career is too important."

He nodded slowly, his gaze focused out the window. "Yeah, you've done well for yourself. It was always important to you."

Important enough that she'd given it as one of the reasons for not marrying him.

"What about you? As the only eligible Walker bachelor left, I'm guessing women are falling at your feet."

He gave her a shrug. "My cousin Todd hasn't gotten hooked yet. I think we're both safe. We enjoy our casual relationships with ladies — no need to get all serious. We're young, successful men. We might as well enjoy our freedom."

The lump in her throat was back, and it threatened to choke her. It was time to change the small talk to something that wasn't going to kill her. She knew he had no intention of hurting her with the conversation at hand. He was being *friendly*. When the wedding was over, he'd go his way, and she'd go hers, just like it had been since she'd walked out of his life. Only now, she had a kind of permission to talk to him as if nothing had ever happened.

She focused on the turn in the road, and the silence between them.

"So, what do you think of the Braves this year?"

CHAPTER 2

The Braves? Gerald shook his head, was that all she had? This woman could stand in a court of law and make the strongest of men shake in his shoes, and she was nervous around him. Wasn't that intriguing?

He didn't answer her. Instead, he turned the radio until he found another song, this one an Elton John classic.

Watching the cars make their first turn from one dirt road to another, he knew they had at least thirty more minutes in the car together. He figured he had a few choices. He could play along and make small talk, or he could continue to make her squirm in her seat. The latter of the ideas was the most intriguing, but no matter what he'd felt for the woman, he didn't seem to think that was fair.

"How are your folks?" he asked, figuring that was safe enough ground.

"Good," she said as she adjusted in her seat. "Dad finally retired, and mom is keeping him plenty busy. I think that's to keep him out from underfoot. Even though she wanted him home, she doesn't want him messing up her house."

Gerald laughed. He'd seen his mother do that with his father and his brothers. She loved to have them around and working the ranch, but she'd rather they did it between eight in the morning and four in the afternoon without tracking through her kitchen.

"Is your dad getting in a lot of fishing then?"

"Oh, you know it. He even booked one of those fishing expeditions in Alaska. I don't eat salmon, but my freezer is full of it."

"And have you talked to Jacob in a while?"

Instantly Ella's chin jutted out, and her shoulders went back. Gripping the steering wheel, her knuckles turned white, and Gerald knew he'd more than likely crossed a line. He wasn't even sure what made him ask, but for some reason the little jab at her made him feel a whole lot better.

"I don't talk to Jacob. That would be where the 'ex' part comes in. I went one way. He went the other."

And, Gerald knew Jacob's way was replacing Ella with a blonde he'd been hooking up with. Wasn't that how he'd heard of their breakup in the first place? He'd run into Jacob at a gas station in Athens of all places. He'd gone to see his cousin Jake race, and while he was checking out with his obligatory Mountain Dew for the day, there was Jacob right in front of him, with his arm around the blonde and his wedding ring still on.

A million things had gone through Gerald's head that day. The first was to haul off and punch the son-of-a-bitch in the mouth. But he didn't have a reason, except that Jacob had been unfaithful to Ella, which pissed him off. Another thought was to put down the damn bottle of green sugar and run to Ella. She was going to need a shoulder to cry on, why not his?

Then he remembered that when he proposed, she'd denied him the pleasure of hearing yes. A few months later she eloped with Jacob, and a few years later Gerald was facing his ex-best friend while the asshole tried to convince him that the leggy blonde, who had been patting his ass was just a cousin visiting from Jersey. It didn't surprise him that Ella moved back to

Macon after that. A part of him thought it was karma, and the other part had wanted to go to her and make sure she was okay.

Soon, the weeks and months slid away from him. He'd buried himself in his work, and for the most part, had forgotten about her. Then Nichole needed someone to represent her, and there was only one lawyer he'd ever trust with his family.

Now here they were, driving down the old dirt roads they used to drive, and they were taking jabs at each other. Okay, he was taking the jab at her, but he needed to. He needed to hear her say exactly what she had. *I don't talk to Jacob.*

"How is your sister?"

He watched her defuse again, just as she had when he'd asked about her parents.

"She's good. Expecting baby number three in a month or so."

"Three? I still think of her as the lifeguard that chased us out of the wading pool."

Ella laughed as the dirt road gave way to the pavement. "She did take her jobs very seriously."

"It runs in the family."

Ella shifted a glance his way and smiled. Once she'd decided to become a lawyer, she'd gone all in. He'd rarely seen her during college because she was so busy. And when it came time to take that lawyer test, she had disappeared entirely from his life, except for the occasional phone call so he could pep talk her.

She'd inherited that work ethic from her father. The man had worked through a heart attack, and then when he was having surgery, he'd set up his office on his bed table. Gerald was glad to hear he was retired and fishing now. It seemed a waste of a perfectly good life to work so damn hard—only to almost die doing it.

Ella turned the knob on the radio, turning down the volume now that the car wasn't on the gravel road.

"I've enjoyed watching your cousins, and sisters-in-law build their businesses at the *Bridal Mecca*. That Lydia Morgan knows how to draw in business, doesn't she?"

"She's incredible. It's a wonder no one has swept her off her feet."

Ella laughed. "When would she have time to date? The woman works all the time. Not only does she run an event center, she's part owner in some brewery, and in her mother's event center too. I'm sure I'm missing some in there." Ella shook her head with a smile. "Ambitious. I've never known anyone like her."

He did, but he was sure she wasn't vain enough to think of herself that way. "If she ever slowed down, maybe Phillip could catch her."

"Officer Phillip Smythe? Are you crazy? She hates him."

Now Gerald laughed. "That's what she says."

"You don't believe it?"

"I'm just saying. You never know what someone is thinking inside. Do you?"

Gerald saw the color hit her cheeks first before her lips tightened. "I have a feeling you have a lot of things you'd like to say to me. You've just been saving up, haven't you? Is that why you wanted me to give you a ride? That way I'd be a captive audience for you?"

"Is that what you think?" Suddenly his anger matched hers, and he hadn't even meant anything by what he said. But she brought it up, well then sure; he'd give her that ear full. "I have a lot to say. Where do you want me to start?"

"Oh, please, start at the beginning."

"You married Jacob." Those were the first words that came to mind and flew from his mouth. They'd start there then.

"I sure did. I married Jacob." Now she reached over and turned up the radio, though he didn't know what good that was doing. Now they were shouting.

"I want to know why you didn't marry me."

"I told you why."

"You gave me a great amount of bullshit about your career and getting settled in that. Fine. I bought that. So what did he offer that I didn't."

"Nothing."

"Then none of this makes any sense."

"And you're hashing out something that is years old."

"Still stings."

She took a breath to say something else, and then her shoulders eased.

"He wasn't you, and that was the selling point."

"Oh, I'm such a bad guy?"

"No," she said, and her voice was soft enough now that she turned back down the volume on the radio. "I couldn't marry you and take you away from the life you knew. Your family needed you, and I needed to do what was right for me. Marrying you would have destroyed one of us."

"Yet we both now live in the same place. Funny how that worked out."

He felt the pang of guilt settle in his belly when he noticed the tears pooling in her eyes.

"I made a mistake, Gerald. I was young, and I needed someone who would blindly let me do what I needed to do."

"When did I not?"

She shook her head and wiped at the tears that now fell. "You always did. You always supported me. Why are we doing this? What happened happened. I gave you up, and I lost Jacob."

"I don't think that was a big loss."

Ella chuckled. "No. It wasn't. Maybe I did you a service taking him out of your life."

He wanted to agree with that, but he couldn't. He'd rather have had Jacob, even on the side as a friend, and have married Ella. But she was right. It wasn't how it worked out, and he was the one suffering by talking about it.

By the time they drove down Main Street toward Lydia's reception hall at the *Bridal Mecca*, the parking lot was full.

"Why don't I just drop you off?" she suggested.

"I can walk with you from wherever you find parking," he offered.

"I think it would be better if I just went home."

That guilt in his stomach grew even more cumbersome. "I didn't mean to…"

"I know. It's for the best, Gerald. I don't think we're quite ready for that friendship we talked about."

And he knew he was to blame for that. He'd been an ass bringing up Jacob and getting in his shots.

Ella pulled up to the curb next to his cousin's hair salon, and he opened the door. "Are you sure you won't come inside? I'll save you a dance."

"I'm sure," she said without even the slightest thought.

Gerald stepped out of the car and lingered with his hand on her door. "I didn't mean to make it awkward. You've done a lot for my brother and sister-in-law. You deserve to be here."

"It was my job."

Gerald gave her another smile and shut the door. As she drove off, he felt a hand on his shoulder and turned to see Lydia watching Ella turn at the stop sign.

"She's not coming in?"

"It seems I have a way with the ladies and it's not a good way."

Lydia threw back her head, her short crop of dark hair bouncing as she laughed. "C'mon, come dance with me. I have a full staff, and I feel like having a few drinks and dancing all night. Besides, Smythe is here, and I don't want him getting anywhere near me."

Gerald laughed as she pulled him toward the door. "Are you sure you don't want him near you?"

Her laughter stopped, and she shook her head. "Never been more sure about anything."

Maybe it was just women. The thought humored him as Lydia pulled him again toward the door. When they made up their mind that they didn't want you, they just didn't want you. There was no reason to spend years wondering why. It was time to move on.

CHAPTER 3

Whea a woman drove away mad, all they wanted was a glass of wine and their best friend, Ella thought as she turned the next corner. Usually, that would work out for her. If she needed something, she'd head over to her best friend Candi's, and they'd watch reruns of *Sex in the City*, drink wine, and eat whatever was in the pantry. But she knew that Candi was at the reception, though she hadn't gone to the wedding.

Now she was utterly alone.

She'd left Gerald at the reception, and she'd seen how Lydia scooped him up the moment Ella pulled away from the curb.

"Serves you right," she said to herself in her car as she pulled up to the ice cream parlor and contemplated a large scoop of chocolate ripple.

Ella sat in her car for nearly twenty minutes before she thought better about the ice cream and backed out of the parking lot. Ordering Chinese takeout, however, seemed like a good solution to her misery. It wasn't any healthier than ice cream or wine, but perhaps more acceptable when she was alone and wallowing in self-pity.

As she set the food on the table, she took a moment to arrange the boxes so it would at least look like a nice dinner. She pulled down a plate from the cupboard and exchanged the wooden chopsticks for a pair her father had brought her from Japan on a business trip when she was a teenager.

Her phone chimed as she filled a glass with ice water. She set it on the table as well as she searched her purse for her phone.

Candi's name flashed on her screen.

Ella gave some thought to whether or not to open the text message as she sat down at the table. Surely it had something to do with the reception. Did she want to go down that road?

What did it matter? She knew she'd given up an excellent time by coming home, but she couldn't be with Gerald in the same room for the entire night. And, likewise, he didn't need her in his space either.

Deciding that she'd read the message, she slid her finger across the screen of her phone to bring it up.

Did you ditch? I saw him in your car. Why is he here and you're not? Next, an image appeared with Gerald and Lydia slow dancing, very closely. His hands were on the small of her back, and she was quite sure Lydia's fingers were in his hair. That seemed a bit intimate.

Didn't think it was a good idea. The drive into town was long enough for both of us, she typed back and set her phone down as she pushed away the plate and went in after the orange chicken right from the container.

She was glad she hadn't stayed. Lydia and Gerald could have an excellent time without her in the way.

Tears burned in her eyes as she took another piece of chicken and shoved it in her mouth. It was stupid to get worked up over it all. She and Gerald had been over for years. She'd married someone else and moved on. There was no reason he shouldn't have moved on too. And if she didn't want to help the Walker family with their legal issues, then she should have picked a different town to move to, because Macon, Georgia was filled with Walkers.

GERALD SUCKED down his third beer as he watched his brother pull the garter from Nichole's thigh. He looked for her sons, wondering what they thought of the spectacle and was happy to see they were huddled in the corner with their sister and his nephew watching something on an iPad.

His cousin Todd grabbed his arm and started pulling him from the safety of his table where he enjoyed the buzz he'd put on.

"If I have to go out there, so do you. There aren't many of us still single," Todd made his bid as he kept a firm grip on Gerald's shirt sleeve.

"I'm coming. I'm coming. You can let go of me now."

"Like hell. I know you'll run because I'd run too."

"Smythe would never let us out the door. Look at him. He's like some general standing there."

Todd laughed. "That's because he doesn't want to do this stupid ritual either."

As the single men gathered on the dance floor, Gerald realized that he and Todd were the last of the Walker men to have to put up with wedding shenanigans like catching articles of clothing pulled from the bride. Gerald had a collection of garters from over the years, but he'd tucked them in a drawer. There hadn't been a woman who even made him think about getting married since Ella had turned him down. In his mind, women were all the same. They thought they knew what they wanted, but they didn't. They wanted to stay home and raise kids, but they wanted a career. They wanted to be equal, but they wanted to be pampered. They wanted to get married, but when you asked them, they turned you down and married your friends—loyal and trustworthy friends.

There were times he thought it served her right to have married Jacob only to have him strut his manhood around to others. But then, he'd always feel guilty for that. He didn't much care for the fact that he'd befriended someone who could be such an ass and do that to his wife, even if his wife had been the one who had broken Gerald's heart and turned him down for marriage first.

Live and learn, he supposed. He wasn't the only Walker man who had proposed to a woman only to have her go off with someone else.

Maybe there was a curse that had been set forth on the Walker men years before he'd been born. One that said all Walker men should suffer first before they were allowed to pull a garter from the leg of their bride.

The thought rolling in his head made him chuckle, just as his brother shot the garter over his shoulder and it hit Gerald right in the chest and fell to the floor.

"Pick it up, sucker," Todd said with a whooping laugh. "Ain't no one else going to touch it."

Gerald shook his head in disgust at his cousin before bending down to pick up the garter that now signified he'd be the next bachelor to tie the knot. But, as he had a drawer full of garters, he didn't buy into the myth.

Realizing his buzz was quickly wearing off, he put the band on his arm and smiled as Lydia sauntered toward him with a beer in each hand. "Dance with me, cowboy."

She handed him a bottle and wrapped her arms around his neck.

When she decided to party instead of work, she let herself be free, he thought as she let her head fall back while she swayed against him.

As he lifted his eyes to those who watched, he couldn't help but notice Phillip Smythe's stern look his way. The man loved the woman who hung from Gerald's neck. The entire town knew it, but they also knew Lydia Morgan couldn't stand the man who seemed to be everywhere she was.

Gerald, on the other hand, seemed to be her flavor of the night. Well, that wasn't fair to her, he thought. She wasn't one to move from man to man, though she did her share of dating. Regardless of the Walker/Morgan dynamic, until his cousin married into the family, Lydia had always been a family friend.

And even as she pressed herself to him in a way he'd never had her do before, he knew that she was just unwinding. He wasn't getting worked up about her hands on him, her breath in his ear or her body pressed to him so hard he feared his body would wake up from a deep slumber and cause a problem.

When the music had died down, and the crowd disbursed to tables to eat more food, Gerald took Lydia by the hand.

"Why don't we go for a walk and get some air?"

She gazed up at him, her eyes clouded from beer and dance. "I could probably use some air."

Gerald kissed the top of her head and walked her out the door past Phillip Smythe's warning glare.

CHAPTER 4

I t hadn't gotten too muggy yet, Gerald thought as he and Lydia walked through the parking lot hand in hand. Georgia could be temperamental with her weather, but the night was just perfect.

"I miss being a guest at parties," Lydia's words swayed with her body.

"Let's go sit on that bench," he offered, steering her toward the bench between his cousins' businesses at the *Bridal Mecca*.

"Maybe I should sell my company so I could be a guest more often."

"You just need to let your staff take care of everything, just like you're doing tonight," he offered as they sat.

"Yeah," she agreed and dropped her head on his shoulder.

He humored himself thinking he was more comfortable outside with a drunk Lydia on his shoulder than he was in the crowded room with family and friends celebrating. Gerald wasn't a crowd-lover. He liked his space. Perhaps that's why he still lived on the ranch and worked alone most of the time.

"Why aren't you married?" Lydia asked, lifting her head, her brown eyes gazing up at him.

"I got turned down, remember?"

"That was a long time ago." Her head dropped back to his shoulder. "You're a good-looking guy. You're nice. You're good looking," she repeated, and he chuckled.

"Thanks."

"I'd marry you in a minute. We could have a whole gaggle of kids, and I'd marry you."

The grin that tugged at his mouth nearly hurt. "Thanks, Lydia. You're good looking and nice too."

"I am. I'm freaking awesome."

"You are."

He wondered how much she'd had to drink, and now that she was pressed against his side, was he responsible for making sure she got home safe and tucked into bed?

"Gerald?"

"Yes."

She lifted her head again and turned, so they were face to face. "Do you like sex?"

The question had him easing back and looking at her. Her cheeks were red, and so were the tips of her ears. Those beautiful brown eyes were glazed over as they looked up at him in a way he hadn't been looked at in a very long time.

"I do."

"So do I. I don't get enough sex."

"That's sad."

"It is sad. I'm too busy. I work too much."

"You love what you do, and you own half the town."

She smiled again and swayed her head from side to side causing him to put his hands on her arms so that she wouldn't fall off the bench.

"I do own half the town. I'm freaking awesome."

"That's what you said."

"Have sex with me." The words came out as though they were

part of a simple conversation and Gerald knew he'd stopped breathing.

"Lydia, you are freaking awesome, but…"

He didn't get the words out before she moved against him and kissed him. But it didn't stop there. She dropped her beer to the ground, and Gerald winced at the sound of it hitting the cement, but not breaking. Lydia shifted and deepened the kiss she was planting on him, and he quickly forgot about the bottle.

God, he was only a man. He wasn't going to take this woman —his friend—to bed, but he sure did like the way it felt to have her lips on his, so he let it continue.

People walked by, and cars drove along the street while she pressed her body against him and moved her mouth and tongue against his.

Now his body had woken up, and to tell her no was going to kill him, nearly. But he would not have sex with Lydia Morgan. No, that wasn't going to happen.

As she swayed back from him, her eyes still closed, she pressed her hands to both sides of her head. "Oh, Lord."

"Yeah."

"No. I'm going to be sick."

He managed to get her to her feet and to a bush at the end of the building before she did get sick. The fringe of her short hair matted to her face as she leaned up against the wall.

"And this is why I work harder than I play," she said before throwing up in the bush again.

"Let me take you home."

"God, everyone saw us, too."

"Yes, and we're going to have to listen to the gossip for months."

She laughed, obviously feeling more sober than before, but still swaying as she looked at him. "Maybe we will have to have sex some other time. I don't think I can do it tonight."

Gerald laughed as he pulled her to his side to help her back to the reception hall so he could drive her home. "Yeah, maybe sex another night would be a better idea."

ELLA'S BOTTOM LIP TREMBLED, and tears pooled in her eyes as she continued down the street in front of the reception hall.

After having sat at home sulking, and receiving Candi's texts, she thought she should suck it up and rejoin the party. But she never would have imagined that as she was looking for a parking space, she'd see Lydia nearly climbing on Gerald as they made out on one of the benches by the street. That was so unlike Gerald to have public displays of affection, and Lydia was usually much too straight-laced to do the same.

What bothered her more was she hadn't seen that coming. She didn't know Lydia and Gerald were an item like that. The few pictures that Candi had sent of them dancing, fine she could almost deal with that. But when she'd seen them kissing on the bench, that took it to another level.

There was no going back into the reception now. She'd drive back home and go to bed. Already she was much too worked up over someone she shouldn't even care about—not in that way.

As she pulled back into her driveway, she rested her head against the steering wheel. The problem was, she did care. Never in all the years that she'd moved on from Gerald did she stop caring about him—stop loving him.

She'd made a mistake, and now she was going to spend the rest of her life regretting that mistake. Deep down inside she knew that was why she'd moved back, even when her parents had moved on. There was an attachment—an unhealthy one—to Gerald, and now she was going to pay for it.

Taking a deep breath, Ella opened the car door and stepped out in her high heels on to the driveway.

She felt like a fraud all dressed up and looking as though she wanted to celebrate a wedding—a new start. The truth was, she didn't feel as though there would ever be joy in celebrating what she'd never had—happiness forever and ever.

Sliding her key into the lock of her front door, she turned it and pushed it open. Quickly, she kicked off her heels and left them on the floor as she walked to the kitchen, poured herself a glass of wine, and plopped down on the sofa. How long was she going to have her little pity party? It was her fault that she didn't get her happily ever after, but when it was offered, she wasn't ready. It was that simple, and she'd be a fool to think otherwise. But damn it hurt to see him exploring his options with someone else.

The wine was bitter on her tongue, and it numbed her brain just enough that she eased back against the sofa, turned on the TV, and for a few moments tried to forget how much it hurt to watch Gerald kissing Lydia. But it didn't last long. She sat back up as other worries crept in.

How had he felt when she'd married Jacob? It had to have felt worse than seeing someone kiss someone else, that was for sure. Did she owe him another apology or was she the only one going through this? It was guilt. She was sure that was what was eating at her.

Finishing up her glass of wine, she pulled the blanket off the back of the sofa and wrapped it around her. They'd hashed it out in the car on the drive to the reception. There was no need for her to continue to hash it out in her mind all night long.

Ella closed her eyes and felt the wine swimming in her head. And as she drifted to sleep all she could see was Lydia pressed against Gerald, and their mouths connected.

CHAPTER 5

L ydia snored softly in the passenger seat of her car. It had
taken him more than ten minutes to find her keys in the
desk drawer of her office, as she wasn't much help.

Somehow Gerald managed to get her to her car without too
many people seeing her being carried out. He'd get her home and
tucked into bed, and then he'd decide how he was going to get
home.

As he drove through town, he humored himself with all of the
businesses that were owned by Lydia Morgan, passing at least
three of them in a two-mile radius. She had her hand in everything. She'd only lived in town about a year, after finally having
moved out of her grandfather's house which was much closer to
his own, down that long dirt road, out where no one else was
around for miles.

There had been times he'd thought about moving to town, but
his life was in the country. The animals, the land, the space—it
was important to him. Any woman he ever married would have
to be okay with living in the country because Gerald never saw
himself tucked in nice and tidy in the city.

He turned down Lydia's street and pondered how someone

who grew up in the country could live in cookie-cutter houses that all looked the same.

She stirred in the seat next to him. "You're home, sweet lady," he said as her eyes slowly opened. "Let's get you inside and tucked into bed."

"I feel like crap."

"Yeah, but I think you had a perfect time at the reception."

Gerald parked the car in the driveway, and helped her out and into the house.

She swayed against him, and there had been a few times where she'd nearly fallen to the floor because she'd fall asleep standing up.

"A few more steps, honey. C'mon," he coaxed her to her bedroom and eased her down to sit on the side of the bed. He pulled her shoes off and helped to lay her back. He didn't know the protocol for sleeping in a bridesmaid's dress, but she could work herself out of that in the morning when she woke.

"You staying to sleep with me?" she asked with her eyes closed.

"I'm going to be on your couch and gone in the morning. I'm a little far from home."

"I'm sorry I asked you to have sex with me." Her words slurred as she pulled the blanket over her shoulders. "You're a good pal."

"Goodnight, Lydia." Gerald pressed a kiss to her temple and then took the other pillow off of the bed, as well as a quilt from the foot of the bed. Leaving the door propped open the slightest bit so he could hear her, he made his way to the living room to sleep on the couch.

He hung his tuxedo jacket on the back of the chair and kicked off his shoes. There was no way he'd strip down to his underwear tonight. Being fully dressed was safer, even if he had no intentions of taking Lydia to bed. But he was a man, and he had to admit that when she kissed him, it stirred up a lot of feelings. They weren't aimed at Lydia, and he knew that much. She was a friend, and even with her tongue in his mouth, he still only felt friendship for her, but he'd missed having someone to kiss.

Gerald shook his head as he made himself comfortable for the night. Perhaps it wasn't Lydia that had gotten him all worked up, no he knew who it was — having that stupid argument with Ella had twisted him up. In the heat of it, he'd thrown all of her mistakes back at her. What an ass he was.

She had her own problems. She didn't need him and his broken heart to be part of that. Besides, they'd moved on to being friends, and that was important, especially if she was going to live in town. She would also still be working with Nichole since her identity was stolen. Even though the woman who had done it was in jail, there still were a lot of things that needed to be taken care of. For his new sister-in-law's sake, he'd take it easy on Ella.

GERALD OPENED one eye slowly and caught the sunlight, but he had a very distinct feeling someone was watching him. When he could, he opened both eyes and turned his head to see Lydia sitting in the chair next to him, her bathrobe on, her short hair wet from a shower, and a cup of coffee balanced between her hands.

"Good morning, sweetheart. Can I make you some eggs?" she asked with a hint of humor.

"Good morning, sweetheart, right back at'cha," he said with his voice cracking. "What time is it?"

"Nine-thirty."

"Damn. For a man who watches the sunrise every morning, this is a whole day wasted." Gerald sat up and stretched. He was going to be sore, that was for sure. "How are you feeling?"

"I'm good. I'm embarrassed, but I feel fine."

"What do you have to be embarrassed about?"

She picked up her phone and turned it so he could see it. Someone had texted her a picture of them kissing on the bench.

"I didn't know we had anyone watching us," he admitted. "Which part embarrasses you? That you were caught kissing someone? Or that you were caught kissing me?"

The humor faded from her expression. "Don't be a jerk. I'm not embarrassed that I kissed you. I'm not even embarrassed that someone took a picture." She studied it before setting her phone back down. "I'm embarrassed that people saw me as drunk as I was."

"You deserve to blow off a little steam too."

"I'm a professional."

"Screw anyone who thinks that your professionalism isn't real just because you had a few drinks."

The smile tugged at her lips again, and that made him feel better.

"Okay, to the next thing then. I'm a little embarrassed that I asked you to have sex with me."

Gerald laughed as he scrubbed his hands over his face. "Oh, honey. If I had a dollar for every woman who asked me for sex…"

She shook her head and picked up a throw pillow, tossing it straight at his head. "I mean it. That was horrible."

"I didn't think so."

"Thank you for being a gentleman."

"That's me."

"It is. But for the record, had you not been one, and we did have sex together, I wouldn't be embarrassed about it or upset. You're a good man, Gerald Walker. I'm lucky to have you as a friend."

Gerald puckered his lips. "So you're saying we could still have sex?"

Lydia rolled her eyes as she stood from her chair. "Offer expired when you fell asleep on the couch. Now, c'mon, I'll make it all up to you by cooking your breakfast and then giving you a ride home. I have to stop by my grandfather's anyway."

He watched her walk away, and he smiled to himself. She'd

have driven him home even if she didn't have to see her grandfather. Lydia Morgan would do anything for him. She was just that kind of friend.

It was inspiring. Well, he'd like to think he'd been that kind of friend last night. He was sorry there were pictures of them doing that—because it did look gross, but he was glad she'd attached herself to him and no one else.

Then he thought about the argument he'd had with Ella, and how he'd made her so angry that she didn't even attend the reception. He owed her an apology for that.

"C'mon," Lydia hollered from the kitchen.

He'd make time to stop by her office and talk to her. But for now, he was going to find out if Lydia even knew how to crack an egg.

CHAPTER 6

C andi had texted and called ten times since Ella had awoken. She wasn't going to answer her, or anyone for that matter. She was taking a mad day, and mad days did not include anyone interrupting her. Mad days also included cleaning her house from top to bottom and usually weeding out her closet. Though the last time she weeded out her closet on a mad day, she'd thrown out one of her grandmother's sweaters that she'd been keeping forever. She wasn't sure why it still bothered her. It wasn't as if she were ever going to wear the darn thing, but she'd wanted to keep it.

With her coffee mug in hand, she watched the news on TV, just putting off the next step of cleaning—the bathrooms. When she'd stripped her bed and put on clean sheets, she'd realized her mad was unwarranted which only pissed her off more. She was headed full on into a mad day over Gerald Walker—again.

There was no reason for her to be upset. She'd offered to drive him to town when he'd asked. She could have left his ass out in the country. There were plenty of people to take him into town, but she'd done it. When he got under her skin, she'd let him.

What if she'd gone to the reception and picked up a date for the night? Hell, she could be waking up with him instead of thinking about Gerald waking up with Lydia.

Just thinking about it pissed her off, and now she was ready to tackle the bathrooms.

By the time the house sparkled, she was ready to call Candi back, but the doorbell rang instead, and she knew Candi had heeded the signs.

"I smell bleach," she said when Ella opened the door. "You've used your mad day well, young one," Candi joked as she pushed through with a bottle of wine and take out that said *Giovanni's*.

"You knew I'd be cleaning?" she asked as she closed the door and followed her best friend to the kitchen to partake in whatever smelled so good.

"You always clean when you're mad. And when you didn't come back to the reception last night after I sent you that picture. And, you've been ignoring me all day. I knew you were mad."

Ella sat down at the kitchen table and watched Candi unpack the bag. "I did come back," she admitted. "I was trying to find a place to park, and I saw Gerald and Lydia making out."

Candi lifted her head and gave her a quizzical look. "Making out?"

"That's what I would call it."

"Gerald and Lydia?"

"Well, yes. You were the one watching them dance all night. Why are you so surprised?"

Candi shrugged as she opened the salad container and set it on the table. "I'm surprised because they're friends—and only friends."

"Then why did you send me a picture of them dancing so close?"

"To make you mad enough to come back to the reception and try and outdo them."

Ella shook her head as she plucked a tomato from the salad and popped it into her mouth.

"Outdo them? Was that in the dancing category or the making out? And who was I supposed to make out with?"

Candi set the container of spaghetti down on the table and followed with paper plates and plastic forks.

"There were plenty of men there that you could have hooked up with."

"Hooking up is not my idea of a good time."

Candi laughed as she sat down next to her. "And that, my dear, has always been one of your problems. If you did hook up once in a while, then maybe you wouldn't be so stressed out." As Ella took a breath, Candi held up her hand. "And don't tell me you're not stressed out. I know you are."

"I have a stressful job."

"And you never have any release."

"I'm not that uptight."

"Just saying you could use some letting go." Candi stood and walked over to the bottle of wine Ella had started the night before. She moved straight to the cupboard with the wine glasses and pulled down two before returning and pouring each of them a glass of wine. "This isn't much, but maybe it'll help."

Ella took the wine. "I'm not that uptight."

"Let's agree to disagree and eat all of this pasta. After we're full, we're going to sit down on the sofa and watch a movie. We might as well drink wine and watch romantic comedies if we've missed your chance to get you hooked up."

Ella pursed her lips, and Candi laughed as she tapped her glass to Ella's.

Shaking her head, Ella sipped the wine. This was why it was good to have a best friend, she thought as Candi began a string of tales from the night before, and not another story had the names Gerald or Lydia.

. . .

WHEN ELLA WOKE MONDAY MORNING, she thought of how nice it was to have the entire house so clean and fresh. She opened the window in her bedroom before she picked out her favorite power suit.

She would be in court the first part of the morning, and later she had a conference call. If the morning went well, she had no doubt the call in the afternoon would be successful. Perhaps she'd try and sneak in to see Audrey and get a haircut at lunchtime. That was if things worked out as planned.

The news on the TV said the stock market opened high. The meteorologist said it was going to be warm, but not so humid. It was stacking up to be a great day.

She deserved a good day after having wasted her weekend depressing herself. But, again on the bright side, she'd cleaned her house and spent the evening with her best friend watching some Amy Schumer movie she couldn't even remember the name of.

When she got to the courthouse, the first parking spot was open. The day was set up fine, she thought as she headed up the steps of the building with her Starbucks coffee in her hand, which the person in front of her had paid for.

"We have a problem," Abe, her assistant, hurried toward her.

Quickly, Ella handed him her coffee, because when he said there was a problem, it meant her entire lovely morning was about to go in the toilet. If he were holding her coffee when he told her the bad news, then she wouldn't spill it down the front of her and ruin her power suit.

"What's going on?"

"The sister of the defendant was picked up yesterday on drunk driving charges."

"So our witness isn't here?"

"Nope."

She let out a long, slow breath. The man she was defending against a hit and run had only one witness to say he wasn't there at the time of the accident, and that was his sister. Otherwise, all evidence pointed to him, even though Ella believed him to be innocent.

"Ms. Mills." She turned when she heard her name only to find the prosecuting attorney motioning for her to join him in the small office to the side of the courtroom.

"Take the coffee with you," she told Abe. "It's a vanilla latte. Drink it."

"Why?"

"I'm afraid it'll end up all over me or someone else if you leave me in charge. Just enjoy."

She followed the lawyer into the room, and he shut the door.

"My client is opting to drop all charges."

Ella eased herself into one of the chairs around the large table. "Why is that?"

"It seems as though we came into some new intelligence on the matter, and we have advised him not to continue on."

She nodded slowly. "Should I have this evidence? If it's exonerating my client..."

"Just take the deal. It's a no harm no foul kind of day."

"So my client wasn't involved?"

"No."

"Maybe I should talk to him and see if he wants to sue for..."

"Ms. Mills, let's just cut all of our losses and walk away."

Her lips twitched wanting to smile, but she refrained. Now she needed to get her coffee back before Abe drank it all.

CHAPTER 7

With Ben off on his honeymoon, in Disney World with his wife and kids, Gerald was picking up the slack. The bonus was he was staying at Ben's house while he was gone. Ah, the bachelor life, he thought humorously as he ate a ham sandwich over the sink taking in his brother's view of the ranch.

The prefabricated house had been the perfect addition to Ben's allotted piece of land. Who could have predicted that he'd fill the house with an entire family in less than a year?

Todd had agreed to help out a little more on the ranch since he, too, had no life. His brother Eric continued to do as much as he could, but with kids now, it made it a little harder to be useful any time of day, especially if his wife Susan had a catering job—and thanks to Lydia, Susan always had a catering job.

Gerald didn't much mind the extra work. He honestly had nothing more to live for than the production that happened on the ranch. He was the last to still live in the main house with his parents. Perhaps he thought he owed them the loyalty since he didn't have a mortgage or rent to pay. Then again, at thirty-one maybe that was the saddest statement of his life.

He was the last of the Walker men on his side to settle down—not for lack of trying. And wasn't it amazing that even in his thoughts everything circled back to Ella Mills?

Washing down the sandwich with a Pepsi he'd found in the refrigerator, he thought about how grateful he was to be spending the week out at his brother's. His mother hadn't had the chance to ask him about not coming home after the wedding. It wouldn't be long before she knew he'd spent the night at Lydia's. It wasn't like she'd scold him and treat him like a child, but having his mother know when he stayed with a woman, sexual or not, was a bother.

He should think about putting a house out on the ranch just like Ben had. They'd each been promised acreage to build on, and Ben had a fabricated house dropped there the year earlier, and it was beautiful. It wouldn't take much for Gerald to do that too.

His chosen piece of land was beyond Eric's on the far north side of the property. The more he thought about it, the more he decided he'd better start making plans. He didn't want to be standing in his brother's kitchen ten years down the road wishing he didn't live at home. If he thought about it hard, he could work himself up into a fury over not having a house and a family to go home to. Yeah, he could hash it out in his head over and over, just as he had done for years. It just wasn't worth it anymore.

As he rinsed off his plate and sat it in the sink, he thought about the pictures that had been taken of him and Lydia. It had been a long time since someone kissed him as she had. The more he thought about it, the more he realized he had enjoyed it. Here he had been spending all his time being worked up over someone who had dumped him and married his friend, and all the while, Lydia had been right there.

Sure, if he made a move on her, Phillip Smythe would probably have him arrested for something. There was no denying the man's feelings for her. However, everyone in town knew how much she despised him.

Maybe he should think more about her retracted proposal. He and Lydia were both good-looking, headstrong people. Why shouldn't they be together?

Then, he thought about Ella, and what an ass he had been to her. Yeah, she deserved it, but it was eating at him enough he knew he owed her an apology. His dad had ordered tires from his cousin Jake, and Gerald was being sent to pick them up in town, so he might as well stop by and apologize to Ella, and then maybe he would drop in and see what Lydia was doing for dinner.

ELLA SAT at her desk going over new information she had on Nichole's identity theft case. They had tracked down all of the open accounts and purchases that had been made under her name. Of course, when someone stole someone else's identity, something else always popped up after the case was closed. But she felt confident that Nichole could go forward with a normal life and not have to worry about the woman who now resided in jail.

In addition to the morning where she hadn't had to be in court after all, and she'd managed to get her coffee back from Abe without even a sip having been taken, she thought it was a great day. And then Gerald Walker slipped through her door, a bag from the deli in one hand and drink carrier in the other.

Nothing came to mind to say. She stared at him, looking all sexy and rugged in his jeans, dirty boots, and his T-shirt marred by something he must have leaned up against earlier.

"Do you have time for lunch?" he asked, his dark eyes shielded by his sunglasses.

"Lunch? Right. Um, sure," she stammered as she rose from

behind her desk and walked toward him taking the bag from him.

Gerald slipped off his sunglasses, and those dark eyes pierced her chest. She'd missed gazing into them.

"If you're too busy..."

Ella shook her head. "Actually, I've had a perfect day, and I'm free," she interrupted as she walked back to her desk and sat down.

"Good." He followed and set the tray with two iced teas, super sweet she assumed, on the desk. "I know I promised not to be a 'drop in' kind of friend, but..."

"It's no problem."

"So why has your day been so good?"

Ella pulled the sandwiches out of the bag and laid them out. "Charges were dropped against my innocent client, and I think we finally have Nichole's case all wrapped up, too."

"Then you're right. It has been a good day." He jabbed a straw through the lid of one of the cups and handed it to her. "I guess this turned into a celebration lunch."

"I'm still curious about there being lunch at all."

Gerald tucked his sunglasses on the neck of his shirt and leaned in, his arms on the desk. "I owe you an apology."

"You do?"

"I was an ass on Saturday, and I'm sorry."

Ella eased back in her seat. "Exactly which part are you sorry for?"

Gerald raised a brow. "I'm sorry I egged you on in the car. You were nice enough to give me a ride, and I poked and prodded until you drove away mad. For that I'm sorry."

She'd genuinely hoped he'd apologize for kissing Lydia too, but that would be stupid. He didn't owe her an apology for that.

Gerald put a straw through the lid of his drink and took a long sip. "You missed one hell of a party."

Ella picked up her sandwich and noticed that she had nearly

squeezed her fingers right through the bread. Easing up, she took a breath. "My evening was just fine."

Gerald picked up his sandwich and took a bite. "Good. What did you do?"

Perhaps she should make up some grand story. Wouldn't he love to hear how she went out, danced, took some stranger home just for the fun of it? The thought tickled her brain, but it didn't reach her heart.

"I drank some wine, watched some TV, and cleaned."

That was when he raised his eyes and met hers. Oh, he understood what it meant for her to say she cleaned. Would he call her out on it? He did suddenly look a little nervous.

Gerald took the napkin and wiped it across his lips. "Then I'm really sorry. If your house is as clean as I assume it is, I made you pretty mad."

She could feel the heat rise in her cheeks. "How come you assume that just because I cleaned it meant I was mad? Perhaps I just like a tidy atmosphere. Maybe, I had planned to go home the entire time. Saturday is usually the day that I clean," she said with her lips getting tighter and her voice rising in pitch. Also, wouldn't he like to know that she been mad long enough that she cleaned all Sunday?

"I didn't come to pick a fight." He opened his hand to emphasize the food on the table. "I brought an olive branch for having started a fight in the beginning. Cut me some slack. I'm just a guy."

That was right, she thought. He was just a guy. Just a guy who carried a chip on his shoulder for her, and she deserved it. Although most guys wouldn't come to apologize to someone they didn't think a lot of, so something told her that deep down inside he still cared for her.

"Thank you for lunch."

"It was my pleasure."

CHAPTER 8

Gerald took his time to drive out to his cousin's garage and pick up the tires his father had ordered. He'd let Jake and his wife, Missy, show him their new race car, and go over it in detail, but he didn't pay much attention to it. His mind was elsewhere bouncing between his sudden desperate need to befriend Ella, and wondering if Lydia was going to think he was crazy wanting to take her to dinner.

As he drove into town, he thought some more about the house he wanted to build. Maybe he'd even buy a camper to put there for the time being. The idea humored him more than he could have imagined. Lydia would have a connection to someone selling a camper he was sure of it. She had the largest network of people he'd ever known.

Gerald pulled into the parking lot behind the reception hall and could hear Lydia yelling the moment he stepped out of his truck. Then, he noticed the police cruiser parked on the street. There was no need to wonder who Lydia was yelling at.

Humored, he slowly walked through the back door and into the dimly lit, empty hall.

"You know that I would never have allowed that to happen." Her voice carried from her office just beyond the dance floor.

"And you were in no position to keep it from happening," Phillip's voice was calm.

"My staff would never serve someone underage. You know the standard I hold them to."

"Lydia, the point is—"

"Take your point and shove it up your—" she stopped short when she saw Gerald standing just beyond the door. "Gerald," she said acknowledging him.

Gerald smiled at her, and then turned a nod toward Phillip. "I didn't mean to interrupt."

He watched the vein pulse at Phillip's temple. "I don't seem to be getting anywhere with her anyway." Phillip turned his attention back to Lydia. "You know this could be your liquor license."

"And if you take my liquor license, I'll go after your badge. I did nothing wrong here, and you know it."

Phillip brushed his fingers over the rim of his hat and then slipped it on his head. "I'll be in touch," he said before walking out of the room.

Lydia fell into the chair behind her desk and pressed her fingers to her eyes. "I swear to God he makes stuff up just to come in here and talk to me."

"What was that about?"

"There was some trouble after the reception the other night. Drunk kids were vandalizing. Someone decided they got drunk at the reception. But not this reception. Not at my location." She fisted her hands. "My servers would never serve somebody underage. I don't care if I was paying attention or not. They would not have done it."

"I'm sure Phillip believes you."

"Sure. That's why he was in here." She stood and paced behind her desk. "He believes me. But who the hell would believe me when I was drunk off my ass? He saw me kissing you out on the street. I'm not sure anybody missed it."

A dinner date wasn't seeming too plausible right now, he thought. "Lydia, I'm sorry."

Her head snapped up, and the crease deepened between her brows. "You're sorry for what?"

"For what happened the other night."

"Did you pour the drinks down my throat? Are you the reason I made bad decisions that night?"

"I don't think you made a single bad decision."

"I didn't pay attention to my business, Gerald." She sat back down and pulled her notebook toward her. "I let my judgment slide that night. I should've been paying attention."

"You should've been having fun at your friends' reception. The reason you have such a great reputation in this town is that you work your ass off. Anyone who doesn't know that is just stupid. You deserved to blow off some steam. You deserve to have some fun. And it is nobody's business who kissed you on the street or who took you home."

Her eyes lifted, and the fury had diffused. "I love you, Gerald Walker. You're a good man."

He thought it was funny that she could tell him she loved him and it sounded just a bit sisterly.

"I want to take you to dinner."

She let out a sigh and shook her head. "Thank you. But I have a lot of fires to put out now. If I find out that one of my servers served somebody underage, that could mean my liquor license. I don't think it happened, but I have to be vigilant in finding out."

"You're sure you don't need dinner?"

Lydia sat forward in her chair and studied him. "I'm going to say this, and it stays right here. Are you trying to build on what happened the other night?"

He opened his mouth to shoot down the idea of what she just

said, but that would be a lie. He tried to think of something, but she laughed and eased back in her chair again.

"Gerald, if that were the case, I would be flattered. Let's say I don't have it in me to start anything with anyone. Though, if that was what you were doing, I consider myself one lucky gal."

And just like that, she had defused the situation in which he had found himself speechless.

"If you change your mind about dinner, you call me."

Lydia smiled at him and then pushed her dark bangs from her forehead. "I'll do just that."

"I almost forgot, do you know anyone who is selling a camper?"

AS EXPECTED, Lydia had a connection to a trailer. A week after having made an ass of himself in her office, Gerald stood on his promised piece of land and examined the vintage Airstream which had just been delivered.

The silver metal shone in the sunlight, and the rolling acreage behind it made for one pretty picture, he thought. He might not even need a real house. He could build himself a little patio, or dig a fire pit and just put chairs around it. The possibilities were endless.

The interior needed a little work, but he was handy enough. Seriously, he never thought that he'd be giddy to move into a camper just to get out of the house in his thirties. And as he looked out over the vastness between his small piece of land and the distance to where his parents' home sat, unseeable from his vantage point, he realized this was a step in becoming an adult, and it was about damn time.

The main house was home. It would always be home. And, had he gotten married years ago, he would have moved out then, but that hadn't happened.

Just like that, he was standing in a field blaming his lot on life on Ella's decision not to marry him—again. If anything made him slightly juvenile, it was holding on to the rejection. She had a reason for what she did. He wasn't the right husband for her at that time. Just because he didn't understand the reasoning behind it, didn't mean it hadn't been the right thing at the right time.

Now he stood there and watched the sun set behind his place —temporary place. No matter how long he would live in the used trailer, he was ecstatic to be on his own.

He saw the dust kicking up on the road. Someone knew where he was and was coming for a visit. Luckily, his first purchase after the trailer was a case of beer and two lawn chairs. It looked like whoever was coming his was going to be his first guest.

Gerald walked into the trailer to retrieve them each a beer.

CHAPTER 9

Gerald looked out the small window over the sink and saw an old pickup truck driving toward him. If he didn't know better, that was Phillip Smythe's truck, though he didn't drive it too often.

Gerald stepped out of the trailer, a beer in each hand, just as Phillip parked the truck next to his, and climbed out.

"Congratulations, you're my first guest. Got time for a beer?" Gerald asked, acknowledging the bottles he held.

Phillip wasn't dressed in his uniform. Instead, he looked as if he, too, had just walked off the ranch. His boots were old and worn, his jeans frayed on the bottom, and his belt buckle proved he'd done more than arrest the low lives in town, he'd held on to a bull or two. His red plaid shirt was tucked in, and the brim of his hat had seen its share of rain and sun.

"Just found out you had a place," he said.

"Lydia let me know of a guy who was selling it when I was looking for something to put out here."

"Time to move out of the folks' house, huh?"

"Yeah. You want to sit down?" Gerald offered, still holding the beer he'd taken out for Phillip.

"No. I came to talk to you, man to man."

Gerald scanned another look over the solemn man who wasn't standing in front of him on official business. Feeling a bit out of place in his own yard, he took the beers, set them on the front step, and crossed his arms over his chest.

"Okay, what do we have to talk about?"

Phillip took off his hat and ran his fingers over the worn fabric of the brim. "Lydia."

Why that hadn't crossed Gerald's mind, he wasn't sure. Maybe it was because Lydia hated the man who seemed so intimidating in civilian clothing.

"She's okay, right?"

"Sure. Sure. I just want to know what's going on between the two of you."

Gerald decided he needed the beer now. He took one, twisted off the cap, shoving it in his pocket before taking a long pull. "What does it matter? Lydia is a grown woman who makes her own decisions."

"She does. She makes a lot of decisions. I want to know what she's decided to do with you."

Gerald ran his tongue over the front of his teeth. "There haven't been any decisions made. I'm not sure what this is all about."

"I'm just asking. I recently found out you spent the night at her house after your brother's wedding."

Gerald was sure that news traveled faster than that. That had been a week ago, and only now Phillip Smythe had a problem with it?

"I took Lydia home after the wedding. She'd enjoyed herself quite a bit, and I offered her a ride."

"But you didn't leave."

"No, I didn't." There was nothing left to say as far as Gerald was concerned. "So, if that's all…"

"Someone dropped me a text with a picture of the two of you

kissing."

Gerald thought about the text that Lydia had also received. "Someone got a lot of mileage out of that picture. Yes, we kissed."

"I just need to know your feelings for her."

"She's a great gal. Phillip, I don't know what this has to do with anything. We kissed the night of the wedding. She got drunk. I took her home, and I stayed. She and I are friends."

"With benefits?" Phillips said under his breath as he put his hat back on his head and adjusted it so that the brim was low on his forehead.

"Are you kidding me? You drove out here to pick a fight with me over Lydia?"

"Everyone knows I would do anything to protect Lydia."

"Yeah, but stopping her from having her own life, that goes a little too far."

He could see Phillip's jaw tighten and his lip twitched. "I'm not stopping her. I'm asking questions."

"And if I didn't break the law then I don't see why you're out here asking."

"What about you and Ella?"

Gerald didn't even have to think about that one before he laughed out loud. "Ella's over me about the same way Lydia is over you," he said, and then wished he hadn't. "Sorry, man."

Phillip tucked his thumbs into the front pockets of his jeans and rocked back on his heels.

"I know how Lydia feels about me. Talk about a woman who can hold on to a mad for a long time—she's your girl. If you're sleeping with her, I just want to know."

Gerald took another long pull from his bottle. "First of all, if I were sleeping with Lydia, it wouldn't be any of your business. Second of all, if she knew you even asked and I discussed it, she'd cut off both of our appendages. And third, no, I'm not sleeping with her. I took a friend home and stayed on the couch. I didn't have my truck in town anyway." He saw some relief come back to

Phillip's face. "And if you're looking for more good news, I tried to stir something up days later, and Lydia isn't interested. I'm a friend. She doesn't want anything to do with me in that way."

"Thanks for that."

"Don't you think you should move on, too? I mean, it doesn't seem like she's warming up to the idea of you being around so much."

Now Phillip smiled and made a move toward the beer on the step. "She's been mad for a very long time. I keep thinking she'll get over it." Phillip twisted off the top to the bottle, tucking the cap in his shirt pocket, and took a long sip. "That's good."

"Why don't we sit in my new chairs and talk a bit."

Phillip nodded, and they each sat in one of the new chairs Gerald had bought to someday sit out by a fire. He wondered what kind of feelings Phillip Smythe must be harboring to drive out to his place to ensure he wasn't sleeping with Lydia. There had been a rumor that they'd had a thing once, Phillip and Lydia, but he didn't remember it. All he could remember was Phillip being anywhere Lydia was, and Lydia trying to go the opposite direction.

Before long, they were two beers in, talking about the *Bridal Mecca*, his brother Dane and his wife Gia's trip to Lucca coming up in the next week and the fact that Eric was looking to expand the house for more kids.

"Time seems to fly by when you add a wife and kids to the mix," Phillip said as he finished off his beer.

"I never thought my brothers would be fathers. Especially Eric. But now, I can't think of anyone who would be a better fit for the job."

Phillip smiled at the thought, and then shifted in his chair as his phone rang and he pulled it from his pocket.

"Smythe," he said as he set his empty beer bottle on the ground next to his chair.

Gerald noted the change in Phillip's expression as he listened to the caller. He watched as Phillip shifted a glance toward the trucks and then cranked his head as if to look at Gerald's truck.

"No other descriptions?" he asked and nodded. "I'll be back in about forty. Get Price moving on a team."

Phillip disconnected the call and stood as he slipped the phone back into his pocket. "This thing have a bathroom?" He nodded toward the trailer.

"Sure, but man, this is the country. Step around back. No one will care," Gerald said with a hint of humor to try and lighten the mood.

"I'm an indoor kind of guy."

"Yeah. Yeah. Go ahead. Just inside. You can't miss it."

Gerald watched as Phillip took off his hat before he entered the trailer, and it was easy to see he was checking out the interior. He'd wished he'd had time to clean it up more before having had his first visitor. Then again, once he was done fixing it up, he could have Phillip out again to show him what he'd done.

A few minutes later, Phillip walked out of the trailer and put his hat back on his head. "Thanks for the beer."

"Something brewing in town?" Gerald asked since the phone call seemed to have put Phillip into a strange mood.

"Yeah. You know the McCarrey family?"

Gerald thought for a moment. "Connor McCarrey was a few years older than me in school. He lives in town and has a family. That's all I know."

"Yeah." Phillip walked to his truck and pulled open the door. Again, he gave a scan over Gerald's truck. "I'll see you around. Thanks for the beer, and if you don't mind, don't let Lydia know I was poking for information."

"I don't have a death wish," Gerald joked, but Phillip only nodded, still preoccupied with whatever had transpired when he'd gotten that call.

CHAPTER 10

Each rut and every bump on that dirt road from the ranch into town had its own story, Gerald thought as the dirt road gave way to the pavement. They'd each put a truck in the ditch more than once when they were learning to drive. The roads that went into the fields had stories of their own too, he mused as he came to the first stoplight in town.

He'd cross a set of railroad tracks, and the town would begin to emerge in front of him, and the fields and ranches would seem distant until he headed back home.

It was a pain in the ass when he had to drive forty-five minutes to get a part he thought he had for a job. It had been the way of life as long as he'd known it. At least they had satellite radio now to keep them company.

Gerald noticed the police car that had pulled out of the 7-11 parking lot and gotten behind him, but he wasn't speeding and his plates were current. He turned up his radio a little more and enjoyed the cruise through town.

It was a beautiful summer day, and the people were walking the quaint stores on Main Street and enjoying ice cream. He'd arrived in town at lunchtime, and the people in their work clothes were headed to restaurants.

Life was much different here than it was on the ranch, but both sides were appealing.

As he turned down the next street, he noticed the police officer was still following him. He only became suspicious when he turned down the next street, and so did the officer.

Did this have something to do with Lydia and Smythe? If the man was going to scare him away from Lydia, he had another thing coming. Lydia had let Gerald know how things were. He didn't need some love-crazed cop pulling rank on him and sending his flunkies after him every time he drove into town.

And, if that was what was going on, Phillip Smythe was going to get an earful.

Gerald pulled into the parking lot of the hardware store and parked his truck on the outer edge of the parking lot, as he could swear they were beginning to make parking spaces much smaller. As he turned off the engine, he noticed the officer pulling in the lot behind him, blocking him in.

The officer stepped out of her car, hand on the butt of her gun, and walked toward his truck as he opened the door to climb out.

"Did I do something wrong?" Gerald asked as he exited his truck. "Was I speeding? Did I go through a stoplight or a sign?"

"This is your truck?" she asked scanning him with her eyes from head to toe.

"Since I was sixteen. Two-hundred-thousand miles on it. All mine."

"It has some front bumper damage to it."

"Sure it does. I live on a ranch. It's towed every kind of equipment you could think of. I feed the cattle from the bed, and they run into it. It's met a tree trunk or two over the years. It's not pretty, but it's a good truck."

"I need to see your license and registration," she said sternly, her hand still resting on her gun.

Gerald reached for his back pocket to pull out his wallet and the officer held up a hand. "Slow."

Christ, this wasn't what he needed. This was harassment, he thought as he pulled his wallet from his pocket and retrieved his license.

He handed it to the officer who kept one eye on him and his license. "Gerald Walker."

"That's me."

"Related to Jake Walker?"

"Cousin."

"Eric?"

"Brother."

She nodded slowly. "Do you have a weapon in your truck? A gun?"

"No, ma'am."

"Why don't you pull out your registration for me as well," she commanded.

He wanted to argue, or even better, walk into the store and get what he needed, but he'd been raised to respect the law, even if he was pretty sure the law was getting back at him for spending the night at Lydia's.

Gerald walked to the opposite side of the truck, the officer standing at the back of his truck keeping an eye on him at all times. He pulled the registration from the glove compartment and handed it to her.

"Stay right here. I'll be back in a moment," she directed as she walked back to her car.

Gerald leaned up against the side of the truck trying to keep his eyes low and not make contact with the people going in and out of the store watching him. This was embarrassing. He'd done nothing wrong. Maybe he should call Phillip and tell him to lay off. Lydia told him no, that was all he needed. This had gone too far.

The officer stepped out of her car and walked back toward him with the items he'd handed her in her hand.

"You check out."

"Good. I was getting nervous. Now, will you tell me what I did?"

"Your truck matches the description in an abduction. A twelve-year-old girl was taken from the mall."

He felt the blood drain from his head. "In a truck like mine?"

She nodded slowly. "You know anything about that?"

"No. No, but I hope they find her," he said honestly. "Who is it?"

"Abby McCarrey. You know her?"

Gerald felt the sickness rise in his throat. That was why Phillip asked him about the family. That was why he was looking around yesterday after he'd gotten the call.

"I went to school with her dad. I don't know Abby. By the way, I was with Smythe when he got the call on the case. I wasn't in town when it happened."

By the look on her face, he decided she already knew that, but she'd pulled him over anyway.

"If I were you, I'd head over and get that on record. Your truck is a match for the description that Abby's friends gave us. Six-foot-two, brown hair, and dark eyes—that's a match too."

"Red, beat-up pickup and a man of my description match a quarter of the men in this town, in all of Georgia for that matter."

"Sure does. So I'd talk to Smythe and get that alibi written down. I'm not the only one looking for an old red pickup with front end damage."

She walked back to her car and drove away, but Gerald stood there trying to breathe. Some rat bastard kidnapped a kid. First and foremost, that was making him sick wondering where she was and what had happened to her. Secondly, he was a suspect.

No matter what happened, or who he'd try and persuade differ-ently when word got out what they were looking for, eyes were still going to turn to him.

He was going to go to the station and have a word with Phillip, but first, he was going to go pick up Ella and take her with him.

CHAPTER 11

Gerald could hear every breath Ella took in the seat next to him as he drove to the police station. She was good and pissed, and she had a right to be. He'd all but forced her to go with him, nearly having to drag her physically from her office, and all because he wouldn't tell her what was going on.

What if she didn't believe him? What if he'd pissed her off enough in the past week or two to make her want to help put him in jail? He couldn't chance it. She'd know what was going on when they talked to Smythe.

Gerald caught her glare when he pulled into the parking lot. "You're turning me in to the police for something?" she asked.

"I need you to go in here with me and talk to Phillip."

"I've seen you talk to the man. You don't need my help. Just because you've got something going on with the woman who hates him, it doesn't include me."

"It's something else." He'd hardly heard the snide remark with the blood pounding in his ears. "Just come in with me, please."

His voice sounded pathetic to him, and it must have resonated with her too by the look that formed on her face.

"Okay. What's going on, Gerald?"

"Let's go in."

GERALD WAS PANICKED, Ella thought as she watched him climb from the truck and head straight for the doors of the station. Something had happened. It wasn't like Gerald Walker to get spooked, and he was spooked.

The door closed before Ella even made it to the front of the building. When she pulled it open, she could see Gerald disappear into Smythe's office.

"I'm here to give you a statement." She heard his voice echo through the lobby as she walked into the station.

Phillip's eyes darted to her as she walked through his door.

"You brought legal counsel? What do you need legal counsel for?"

"I'm legal counsel?" she asked looking at Gerald. "That's why you dragged me over here?"

Phillip clicked his tongue against his teeth. "So you're not here on your own accord? Mr. Walker forced you to come here?"

"Well..." she stammered as Gerald held up a finger.

"You know damn good and well why I have her here with me," Gerald said. "You have a beef with me, and you have your force hunting me down when you know I'm not guilty of anything but spending the night at Lydia's."

Ella heard her own gasp as she choked on her breath. She could feel the tears stinging in her eyes, and they were unwarranted. There was no reason she should care who he slept with, but hearing it come from his mouth hurt.

"I'm not petty enough to send my deputies after you over something like that, and you know it," Phillip said as he stood from behind his desk. "Your truck matches the one we're looking for."

Ella stepped between the men. "Let's stop right here." She turned to Gerald. "You have me here so you can confess?"

"Hell no!" His voice was loud and shot through the room. It must have stirred someone in the lobby because she saw Phillip's hand rise as if to stop someone from coming toward them. "I didn't do anything, and he knows it. I was with him when he got the call."

She turned to Phillip. "What call?"

"Abby McCarrey disappeared yesterday afternoon. Witness, her nine-year-old sister, and a friend described the truck and the man. He's a fit for all of it."

"You know better than to think it would be Gerald," she argued.

Phillip hooked his thumbs into his front pockets. "I had a deputy that went after his cousin and shot his brother and burned his house down because he was insane. Not everyone is cut and dry."

"Well he is," she continued. "You know that. I know that. And I'll bet if you ask the McCarrey's, they know that, too."

"And how many kids are abducted by uncles, teachers, and parents? He's as much a suspect as anyone."

She could see Gerald's hands ball into fists at his side, so she moved toward the desk, resting her hands on it and leaning in toward Phillip.

"Then my client is here to make a statement and secure his alibi."

Phillip gave her a slow nod. "I think that's a good idea."

PHILLIP HAD LEFT the office to secure a room to get his statement in. Gerald was no criminal, and he refused to have anyone, even Phillip Smythe, think he was.

Ella paced in front of him, biting on her thumb. She'd come to his defense even if she didn't know why she was there. She believed in him, and that came through when she spoke to Phillip.

"Thank you," he said, breaking the suffocating silence between them. "I should have told you why I needed your help, but I was in a hurry to get this over with."

"I would always help you. You know that."

Well, he'd hoped for that.

Ella turned and held up a finger as if in thought. "You spent the night at Lydia's?"

He'd like to punch Phillip for Ella getting that information, but he remembered it was him that said it out loud.

"I took her home after the wedding reception since she'd had too much to drink. I slept on the couch since it was late."

"The couch?" Ella crossed her arms and stared at him with eyes that could slice skin.

"Believe what you want to believe. Lydia is my friend and only my friend."

"I saw you two making out on the bench outside Pearl's bridal shop. That wasn't just a friendly kiss. That was *hurry home and jump in bed if we can make it out of the car* making out."

Gerald ran his fingers over his brow. "You saw that?"

"Yeah."

"And that's why you were cleaning?"

She dropped her arms, and Gerald took a step back. He knew what was coming.

"It's your business," she spat out.

"Yeah? Then stop asking about it."

"Do you want my help here or not?"

Gerald let out a breath and relaxed his shoulders. "Yes. I need your help. I didn't do anything wrong. I also didn't sleep with Lydia. I slept on the couch because it was late, and she was drunk. I wasn't at the mall yesterday, and I didn't abduct any kid either."

"I know," she said softly.

"Which part?"

"I know it all. I believe you, and I know Phillip does too."

"Point is, I didn't do this, but someone did. That little girl is still missing, so it's not about me in the end, it's about her. Once I'm out of here, I'm going to help look for her. I know this area better than anyone."

They both turned when they saw Phillip standing in the door. "No need. They found her—safe," he added, and Gerald thought he might just burst into tears.

When he turned and looked at Ella, her eyes had gone wet.

"Where?" Gerald asked.

"A bus stop in Athens. They're getting more information now. She doesn't seem harmed, only scared. We'll see what comes to light when she gives her statement. Her parents are headed to Athens now."

Gerald took a moment to take in the news. "I'm glad she was found. Do you still need my statement?"

Phillip nodded. "Yeah. We don't have the guy in the truck yet."

"Okay, I'm ready."

Phillip turned and walked down the hall, and Gerald and Ella followed.

The emotions that stirred in him had him sick. There was worry, anger, and joy that she'd been found. It was too much for a man who liked his solitude and his country surroundings.

Ella walked beside him, her small five-foot-two shadowed by his six-foot-two, yet he feared her as much as he loved her. And that revelation shook him even more.

As if she'd known what he was thinking, she looked up at him, her eyes dry now but red. She gave him a soft smile, and slid her hand into his, squeezing it.

Things were different again. Where could this possibly lead?

CHAPTER 12

The afternoon dragged on as Phillip asked Gerald questions about his whereabouts when Abby McCarrey had been abducted. He also added to the video that he was with Gerald when he'd received the phone call and that he'd been given permission to go into Gerald's house.

Ella had seen Gerald's face turn red when Phillip added that bit of information, but he didn't argue it. Under the surface, they were friends, and this would pan out, Ella thought as she took her notes.

When they'd been released, she thought Gerald looked as though he'd been through an emotional ringer, and why? Because he had a beat-up red pickup? Or because he'd slept on Lydia's couch?

Either way, he'd done the right thing, and maybe any harassment of him would stop.

As they walked out to the parking lot, she remembered he'd abruptly picked her up at her office. But looking at him, she didn't think he should be left alone just yet.

"Could I interest you in an early dinner?"

Gerald scrubbed his hand over his face as he pulled open her door. "I need to get these tires to my Dad. This trip wasn't supposed to take all day."

Slowly she nodded as she climbed into the truck and he shut the door.

When they were on the road, she turned in her seat. "You're sure the tires can't wait? There's a new German place in town I've been dying to try."

A smile formed on his lips, but he shook his head. "Nah. I'm just not up for crowds."

She couldn't blame him. In one day he'd been targeted and accused—and she'd done some of the accusing. But deep in her heart, she'd known he'd never done anything wrong—and she knew nothing had happened with Lydia too.

She might have left the man and broken his heart, but she'd never stopped caring for him. People made mistakes, and she'd made a doozy. So, the fact that he wanted his peace and quiet, which was always his way, she respected that.

Gerald pulled up next to her car in the lot, which was mostly empty now.

"Thanks for being there for me," he said looking out the front window. "I didn't know if I could keep my cool with Phillip or not."

"I'm glad you trusted me enough to take me. And you're sure about dinner?" she asked again.

He nodded. "I'm sure."

She wanted to lean over and kiss him, but she refrained. "I'll talk to you soon," she said, and Gerald smiled as she exited the truck.

Once she had climbed into her car and driven away, then Gerald drove the other direction. A gentleman, she thought. He'd never leave until she was safe. A man like that wouldn't hurt a child. A man like that wouldn't hurt anyone.

A man like that would take a drunk friend home and sleep on

the couch she told herself as she drove to the pizzeria down the street from the *Bridal Mecca*.

He might not have wanted to be in public with her, but Ella wasn't done spending time with Gerald yet.

She went inside and ordered a double pepperoni pizza and then went down the street for his favorite beer. The pizza would be cold long before she made the drive out to his house, but it would be worth it.

GERALD FIGURED the next thing that would happen to him would be a speeding ticket because he couldn't get home fast enough.

He'd taken the tires to the barn out by Eric's house and texted his father that they were there. The quicker he could get in and out of places the better. That rundown trailer was a sight for sore eyes.

There were fresh tracks in the dirt he noticed as he'd pulled up. No doubt Phillip had someone out there snooping around while Gerald was in town. No need to get worked up over it, he thought as he put the truck in park and killed the engine. They'd found Abby McCarrey, and they'd done so by looking. At least by searching around, they knew he was on the up and up.

As he climbed from his truck, he heard the sound of tires on gravel coming up the road. That anger that had been boiling in him all day rose to his chest. If Phillip had sent one of his brothers out to talk to him, he'd punch whichever one showed up. He wasn't in the mood for people.

Gerald stepped to the back of his truck and watched as the familiar BMW wound around the corner and into sight. He certainly hadn't expected that.

Ella parked next to his truck and stepped out of her car. "You got set up on your part of the land, huh?"

"How did you know where this was?"

Ella smiled. "I didn't. I stopped by the main house, and your mother told me. She said I could come right out. I brought pizza and beer, but the pizza might need a warm up."

"I thought I said I didn't want to go to dinner."

"We're not. We're having dinner here," she offered, but her smile twitched now. "I thought you looked like you might need company after today."

"Maybe I needed to be alone."

Her eyes went sad, but the smile remained. "Okay. Well, here," she said as she leaned into the car and took out the pizza box and the beer. "You might as well enjoy these."

He couldn't stand to see her standing there like that. Something had to be done.

Gerald moved to her, and she backed against the car. Her eyes had gone wide, and perhaps he'd startled her a bit.

"What are you really doing out here?"

Ella swallowed hard and shifted a glance between the pizza box and the beer. "I just thought you could use some dinner."

Gerald moved in even closer, resting his hand on the top of the car over her shoulder and pinning her there with the proximity of his body.

"What are you doing here?"

"Gerald, step back."

"Ella..." He could see her mouth tremble now. "Why did you come out here?"

She hesitated for a moment, collecting her thoughts, he assumed. With a flush coloring her cheeks, she lifted her eyes to meet his. "To be with you."

"You don't like me," he teased as he kept his eyes on hers. "Tell me why you're here."

"You're being an ass."

"Always. Tell me."

"Gerald, I'll go. Just..."

He took one more step closer, closing the distance completely. "Tell me."

"I want to be with you," she said, and her voice was airy and sexy, and it hit him in the chest.

He took the pizza and beer from her hands and turned. He walked toward the trailer and smiled when he heard her car door slam.

"Seriously? That's how you're doing this? You are an ass."

"I didn't say I wasn't," he called back over his shoulder and caught sight of her running to him, her hands balled into fists.

He turned in time to put the pizza and beer on the hood of his truck, just as she came at him with all that fury.

He caught her hand before it hit, and then the other. Directing her around, he had her back against his truck, and he dove in to take her mouth with his because he couldn't stand not to one second longer.

CHAPTER 13

Ella managed a breath before his mouth came back down on hers and Gerald's tongue slipped through to dance with her own.

With her hands still fisted against his chest, and her body rigid beneath his.

When Gerald's fingers moved into her hair, just as they had once before—a long time ago—her body eased, and her fists opened and gripped hold of his shirt.

She pulled him even closer, forcing him to deepen the kiss that had already sucked her in.

Was this what she'd wanted? Was this the reason she'd driven out there uninvited?

She'd missed him—every part of him. Regret for what she'd done to him sunk into her belly. This could have been hers the whole time. She could have been his, but she'd given that up—and why? What had made his offer to marry her seem so unimportant?

Ella pushed back and took a breath.

"I'm sorry."

Gerald's breath was thick on her cheek. "Sorry? God, for what?"

Ella moved out from under him and paced a small circle. "How can you ever forgive me enough to welcome me into your home—or your life?" She pressed her fingers to her temples. "Why don't you hate me?"

Gerald's mouth had dropped open as he stared at her. "I've never hated you."

"But why? You should have thrown me off your land by now, but you didn't. I came back to town single—which meant everything I did failed, but you didn't treat me unkindly. None of you did. Instead, when your family needed help, you came to me."

"I'm not getting what you're trying to say. Do you want me to hate you?"

"It would make more sense than you kissing me."

Gerald rubbed his fingers over his chin and leaned up against his truck. "We were kissing, right? I mean you were part of that, right?"

"Don't make fun of me."

"I'm not," he snorted as he moved from the truck and walked toward her. "I wasn't brought up to hate. You know that. I was brought up to forgive and move on. I forgave you for dumping my ass a long time ago. I moved on. You moved back."

"And now we're kissing. Where does that lead?"

"I don't know, Ella. All I know is that when my family needed you, you were there. When I busted into your office and said follow me, you did. You didn't know what I needed, but you were there to help. And here you are, pizza and beer in hand. It looks like we've put our differences aside, doesn't it?"

"I hate me," she admitted. "I hate what I did to you."

"Hating what you did to me, and hating yourself are two different things."

God, why did he always make sense? Was that a Walker thing? They were born with insightfulness, she decided.

"You're right. I hate what I did."

"Then don't do it again," he finished before he swiftly moved to her and scooped her legs out from under her, carrying her up the stairs and into his trailer.

No, she thought as he kicked open the door, she would never do it again.

THE TELEVISION FLICKERED LIGHT against the walls of the trailer in the dark where Ella rested against him, wrapped only in a blanket and eating a reheated piece of pizza. How had the day come to her in his arms, naked, and utterly content with being there? Had they fallen back into what they'd lost years ago? Or were they both so desperate to feel something that they were using each other? It killed him that he didn't have an answer for that. He wasn't sure of his feelings, how could he even pretend to guess hers.

"Are you going to live in this trailer forever?" she pondered as she put her plate on the folding table next to the couch.

Gerald shrugged. "It was a good buy for now. Ben had one of those prefabricated houses put up on his land, and I'm considering that too. Eric built his house after it burned down."

"I heard about that fire. About all of it—the crazy cop and how he was obsessed with Bethany. How traumatic."

She'd heard. She hadn't reached out, but she kept her ear to the ground.

"That's all behind us. It's been a crazy few years. I suppose that's why I like the trailer. It's just simple and peaceful. It doesn't make any flashy statement. It just sits out here and waits for me to sleep."

Ella moved against him, her hand coming to his bare chest. "And I'm the first girl you've had here?"

This was the start of a slippery slope, and he knew it. She was fishing for answers in her lawyerly way.

"I've had exactly two visitors who weren't family," he began and thought about the tracks he'd seen when he arrived. Perhaps he'd had more visitors—uninvited. "You and Phillip. And though Phillip took a moment to come inside and look around, I can't say he was invited."

"I wasn't invited either."

"Well, let's just say there is an open door policy for you," he offered as he pressed a kiss to her forehead. "I'd like to see you in my house a whole lot more."

"I'd like that."

"Would you?"

Ella shifted so that she was eye to eye with him. "I never stopped feeling for you. I think it made everything harder."

He'd felt the same, but he thought he'd hold on to that information just a bit longer.

Ella tucked a stray hair behind her ear. "I wanted to call you a million times before I moved back, but I panicked. Even when I did move back, if I saw you or anyone from your family, I hid. Once, I saw Russell and his son walking down the street, and I hid in a hardware store. I couldn't have imagined that your entire family would have been nice to me."

"Then you didn't know us at all."

"But I did. I was hiding from myself." She lifted her hand to his stubbled cheek. "I couldn't have imagined this was where I would land."

"Invitation holds. Anytime. You can guarantee there will be no one else out here wrapped in my comforter."

Seductively, she licked her lips. "No one?"

"No one."

"Lydia?"

"Don't start that again."

A smile formed on her lips as she inched closer. "I think you made your point on that. I'll stop asking."

"Thank you."

"I'm kinda tired. You up for an overnight guest?"

He studied her in the light of the television. There wasn't a part of her that he hadn't committed to memory and dreamed of every night. "I'm up for it. You in need of getting any sleep?"

Ella bit down on her bottom lip and shimmied off the couch, letting the comforter drop to the floor. Brushing her hair over her shoulder, she walked toward the back of the trailer, and he watched every graceful moment until she disappeared.

God, he hoped they'd mended fences and were on their way to becoming one again. If not, it was going to hurt like hell—even more so than the first time.

CHAPTER 14

S unlight—was that really sunlight?

Gerald rubbed his eyes with his free hand and chuckled when he realized his other hand was tucked under Ella and tingled with sleep.

He couldn't remember the last time he'd slept in long enough that the sun made it up before he had. No doubt he'd catch hell over it from his brothers. In fact, he was surprised his phone hadn't been ringing like crazy. Then he remembered, he'd left it in his truck. As he kissed Ella on the forehead, he was thankful that his evening hadn't gone the way he'd wanted it to. He had planned to lock himself in his little mobile house and drink himself to sleep. He had to admit, having Ella in his arms all night had certainly shifted his attitude.

Gerald realized his dreamy morning was over when he heard the tires on the gravel. Which brother was arriving to bust his chops? When Ella sat straight up in bed, pulling the bedsheet up around her, he realized she, too, had heard the vehicle pull up outside.

"Someone is here," she fretted, kicking her legs over the side of the bed. "Where are my clothes? Someone is going to see my ass."

He didn't mean to laugh, but he couldn't help it.

"The door is locked. No one is going to see your ass, but it's a nice sight."

Not amused, he thought, as she found pieces of her clothing scattered around the room.

Gerald swung his legs over the side of the bed and pulled on his jeans just as the pounding started at the door.

"Walker! I know you're in there!" Phillip Smythe's voice rattled through the trailer. "Get out here."

"Crap. What the hell does he want?"

Gerald walked through the trailer and forcefully pushed open the door.

Phillip stood at the bottom of the steps. His hat low over his brow and his hand on the butt of his gun.

"You thinking about using that on me?" Gerald snapped.

"I might. Get out here."

"I thought we finished our business yesterday."

Phillip's lips pursed. "I thought so too."

Gerald stepped out of the trailer, closing the door behind him. The coolness of the morning nipped at his bare chest.

"Sleeping in?" Phillip scoffed.

"What does it matter?"

"I see you had a guest."

"Maybe I did."

"We have another witness saying they saw a truck with your description, and we have another girl missing."

Gerald felt the sickness stirring in his stomach as he had the day before. "Phillip, you know I didn't do that."

He watched as Phillip's expression eased. "In my gut, I know that. One witness gave us a few digits of the plate. Same digits on yours too."

"There are only so many combinations of letters and numbers."

Gerald didn't turn when he heard the door open behind him. He watched as Phillip eased his hand off the butt of his gun, pulled off his hat, and held it in his hands.

"Ella."

"Phillip," her voice floated from behind Gerald.

Gerald tucked his hands into his front pockets. "I have an alibi. You can question her if you'd like."

Phillip put his hat back on and lifted his head to look at Ella. "You were here all night?"

"All night."

"When did you get here?"

"I left the station, got a pizza and some beer, and came straight out."

Phillip nodded. "You two patched things up, huh?"

Gerald clucked his tongue. "It looks like we have. Listen, I don't know why someone turned in my truck. It's been sitting here since I drove it home. But who is missing?"

"Sara Crow."

"Don't know her," Gerald said as Ella walked down the steps to stand beside him.

"I do." Ella admitted. "She's a receptionist in my building. Twenty-something. Short, dark hair. Gaelic tattoo on her wrist."

Phillip ran his hand over the back of his neck. "Yes. That's her."

"Where was she?"

"Grocery store. Had just loaded her car when the red pickup pulled up."

Gerald looked at Ella standing next to him dressed in the suit she'd had on when she arrived. Her hair mussed from sleep in his bed.

"If it was so public, there has to be surveillance footage," she offered.

"There is. It looks just like Gerald's truck. Witness gave us part of the plate, but it's got one of the covers on it, just like yours, to avoid speed cameras."

Gerald's lip twitched when Phillip called him out on the cover.

"The number matched Gerald's?" Ella asked.

"Part of it. All we can get is the truck on the video."

"And you can see the driver in the cab of the truck?"

"No," Phillip admitted. "And that's the biggest problem."

"I can guarantee you that Gerald was here with me all night long, Phillip. Whatever is going on with this guy, is a coincidence."

"That's a pretty big one."

"Might be, but my client doesn't have to answer any more of your questions unless you come with a warrant."

"Your client," Phillip snarled and shook his head. "I'll be back with one if I need one."

"You're not going to need one," she assured him.

Phillip tipped his hat to her and walked back to his car, making sure to take one more long look at Gerald's truck before he drove away.

"That man is going to drive me over the edge," Gerald admitted as the dust kicked up on the road.

"Do you think he's targeting you over Lydia?"

He would have taken a jab at her over the comment, but there was a different look to her as she watched Phillip drive away. She was serious now—lawyer-like.

"No. I think he's got a problem in town. Only I have a problem with the guy causing the problem."

When she turned, the seriousness of it all darkened her eyes. "You need to stay out here. Keep away from town. I'll come back out tonight. Tell your brothers what's going on in case they know of something."

"I'm a grown man," he reminded her. "I don't need some little woman to stand up for me."

This time she rested her fists on her hips and narrowed her gaze. "Well, if they arrest your sorry ass you'll need this little woman to stand up for you. You're not guilty of anything, Gerald Walker, and I'll defend that to the grave. Now, a woman is missing who works in my building. Someone has her, and someone is devastated because she's gone. I can be more helpful to the community if I head to town."

Once she was done, he was deflated, just as he assumed she wanted him. He'd fall in line, just as she wanted. It hurt his masculinity, but she was right, and he knew it.

"I have a fence to fix, a calf to tend to, and it's my turn to gather eggs. I'll be too occupied to cause any problems."

She gave him a curt nod. "And if problems come your way, you call me."

"Yes, ma'am."

He heard the long breath she took in and expelled out as her shoulders dropped. The stern look was replaced with a soft smile as she moved to him.

"I very much enjoyed my night, Gerald. Above all else, I wanted you to know."

Placing his hand on her cheek, he lingered there before leaning in for a kiss. "I'll see you when you get back."

"I look forward to it."

CHAPTER 15

The entire drive into town, to her house to get ready, and into the office had been silent. Ella hadn't turned on her radio or queued up a podcast. No, all the noise was in her head, and she couldn't make sense of any of it.

Was Gerald being targeted, or was it all coincidence? She'd passed four—four—red, beat up, farm pickups on her way into town. Surely they were all being questioned as well, right?

She'd ask Phillip. He owed her that much.

Though Sara hadn't been at work when she'd been abducted, police presence was noticeable at the building where Ella worked. She wasn't sure if she should feel more secure having them around, or if there had been leads that centered around the building.

Either way, she had work to do. Gerald Walker wasn't the only person she had on her defense docket.

She'd gone straight into her office and shut the door when she'd arrived. It hadn't even been an hour when someone knocked, and the receptionist escorted Phillip Smythe in.

"You didn't get enough information this morning?" she asked and irritated herself at the bite in her words.

Phillip stood in front of her, his hat in his hands, and his fingers were running across the brim.

"Sara Crow was found this morning."

Ella felt the air whoosh from her lungs as she sat back in her chair. His demeanor didn't lead her to believe that the rest of the news was going to be good.

"Where?"

"Outside Athens, just like the other."

"She's okay?"

Phillip sat down in the chair across from her and shook his head. "They found her alive. Side of the road. Beaten." He tossed his hat on her desk and ran his fingers through his sandy hair. "She died from her injuries about an hour ago."

"Oh, Phillip." Ella leaned in, resting her arms on her desk. "This is horrible."

"They don't think she was sexually assaulted, and Abby wasn't either."

"Someone just gets a thrill out of kidnapping?"

He shook his head again. "I think we have something bigger. He—I assume he—is feeling this out. Abby and Sara were similar in height and look. I think he's going a little farther each time."

"You think there will be more?"

"I hate to say that."

"I hate it too." Ella crossed her arms in front of her, suddenly chilled by his words. "What do you need from me?"

"Tell me it's not Gerald, and I'll leave it all alone."

"You can't do that. You know that." She shook her head. "It's not Gerald. I was with him last night, all night. And you were with him when they called in the missing girl. You know it's not him."

"Yeah, but the Walkers have some serious crap luck with things like this. Look at Eric and Bethany. He lost his house and got shot over some crazy lunatic. Russell got run off the road by another. The list goes on and on."

"You think someone is setting him up?"

Phillip eased back in his seat. "I don't know. I can't tie it together. He's taking girls from here and dumping them in Athens. There's no correlation, except that the truck is a match and so is the description of the man, though vague."

"It's not enough to go on."

"No. But I'd throw Gerald's ass in jail to keep him safe," Phillip admitted, and it brought Ella some peace. "Tell him to park that POS truck and drive something else from the ranch. That'll keep him under the radar in town."

"Okay."

"And you watch your step," he warned as he stood and gathered his hat. "This guy is around, and I don't want anyone to get hurt."

"I'll be careful."

"I'm headed over to the *Bridal Mecca* to talk to the ladies there. Seems like a prime target to me."

"I wouldn't want to be the guy who messes with one of them."

That made him chuckle. "It's not great to be on the wrong side of them."

She figured he would know.

"Take care, Ella." He turned to leave and stopped at the door turning back to her. "Gerald is a good man. I'm glad you guys worked it out."

"Me too."

Phillip's visit should have brought her some comfort, at least his admission that Gerald was a good guy. But it seemed to have had the opposite effect on her. Who was this creep? Why was he stalking women? Gerald just was an ordinary guy, and that was this guy's cover, right? Regular Joe?

She swiveled in her chair to look out the window. Every person on the street had a different story. They came from different backgrounds and chose different paths. Watching, she noted that every man on that street below her office had some trace of Gerald. Height, weight, jacket, hair color, and swagger. Could it be that the only thing keeping Gerald as a suspect was that stupid truck?

Pressing her hand to her belly, she fought off the wave of doubt that made her sick. It was all coincidence. Gerald could never do anything so horrible as to kidnap a woman or a child.

She shook the thought from her head. No, Gerald would never do anything to harm anyone. She was more capable of hurting someone than he was.

Her mind went to Sara Crow, who was dead now. Tears stung her eyes, and she closed them to ward away the pain that it caused her. Whoever had taken her had discarded her. She agreed with Phillip's assessment. Whoever was doing this was working up to bigger things.

Ella didn't fit his profile. For that, she was grateful but no less scared. What if he took these women for looking one way, but decided that she fit the bill with her blonde hair and small frame?

Her hands shook, so she clasped them together atop her desk.

When the phone on her desk buzzed, she jumped. Her heart hammered in her chest, so she pressed her hand to it.

Picking up the phone, she noticed her hand still shook.

"Your one o'clock just arrived." Abe's voice cheerfully filled her ear.

"One o'clock?" She looked down at her wrist and realized she hadn't charged her watch since she'd slept at Gerald's. How had the day passed so quickly? "Okay, send them in."

The rest of her day was spent listening to the angry high-pitched voice of a woman scorned by her husband. Every time Ella had thought they'd managed to settle the case against him, the wife—ex-wife now—wanted something else. Ella listened to her demands, talked her out of some, and listed the others. She would make the call to the husband's—ex-husband now— lawyer in the morning and they would begin working through a settlement—again.

By the time the woman left, Ella was mentally and physically exhausted. Why would someone want to get married, only to... she stopped right there with the thought.

She, of all people, had no right to wonder why someone would marry someone else—or not marry someone.

What she did know was she'd spent the night in the arms of the man she'd never stopped loving, even if her emotions had gotten in the way of that love. Of course, she wasn't stupid enough to think that it wasn't just sex either. It was entirely possible that Gerald Walker would turn around and say, "Ha! That was for what you did to me years ago."

Anger rose from the pit of her stomach before she could let the thought go. Gerald wasn't like that. If he wasn't interested in furthering a relationship with her, well that was his right.

Ella buried her face in her hands. She was just worked up. A lot was going on, and she had a lot on her mind.

The knocking at the door had her lifting her head as Gerald walked through.

"Still here, huh?" He smiled at her as he closed the door behind him. "I was hoping I'd catch you. I thought we could go to dinner and stay at your place."

She was sure her expression must not have been what he'd expected. She stared at him in disbelief. "You came to town for that?"

"I borrowed dad's SUV."

Tears stung her eyes and laughter contradicted the feelings stirring in her.

"I had just talked myself into thinking last night was just sex. You and me rekindling something we understood."

"Why would you say that?" He moved toward her desk. "That's not my style."

"Not mine either," she admitted looking up at him. "I was working on a divorce case, and it just got in my head. It made me realize a lot of time has passed for us. What were we thinking last night?"

Gerald walked around her desk, took her hand, and pulled her from the chair. "Your overthinking cost me, last time, and I'm not sorry for saying it like that. I carried you into my place last night full of pent up emotion for you, but you didn't fight it or run away. You were the one who came to my defense and then brought pizza. So don't go overthinking this either," he concluded before he pressed his mouth to hers and solidified his point.

CHAPTER 16

He hadn't driven into town for her to meet him with resistance. Ella Mills was on his mind from the time he woke up with her until he'd pressed his mouth to hers.

Now she took from him, just as he'd have expected. Ella's fingers gripped his hair, and her tongue worked against his. Gerald pulled her as close to him as he possibly could. He wasn't about to let her mind wander into territory that would make the feelings he was having impossible. He'd never stopped loving her. There were reasons Ella had come back to Macon. Gerald wanted to be one of those reasons.

When they'd had their fill, Gerald eased back and rested his forehead against hers. "Let's get some dinner, have a glass of wine, and some easy conversation. Then we'll stay the night at your place if that's okay."

"It sounds perfect."

He wanted to tell her he loved her, but even if they had shared the words in the past, he knew it wasn't the right time to say them. Holding on to them in his heart, he waited for her to gather her things.

As she picked up her purse and her bag, she looked up at him. "Have you talked to Phillip today?"

"Just this morning when he drove out to accuse me again. Why? What did I miss?"

"Sara Crow died this morning from her injuries."

He felt the blood drain from his head and he reached for the back of one of her chairs to support him. "Son-of-a-bitch!"

"He said she hadn't been sexually assaulted, just kidnapped and beaten."

"And left for someone to find?"

"Yes."

Gerald scrubbed his hand over his face. "We have to get this bastard. We have to pool resources and get him."

"Phillip is hell-bent on doing so. He told me to be careful, and he headed from here to the *Bridal Mecca* to talk to Lydia, your cousins, and sisters-in-law."

"It makes me sick."

"Me too," she admitted as she swung her bag over her shoulder. "For tonight, let's have dinner and enjoy a quiet night in."

Ella reached her hand out to take his.

Maybe it was the right moment to tell her he loved her. What if tomorrow never came?

His thoughts were diverted when her phone rang.

"Hello, Mama. Yes, I'm okay. I know, I know," she said as she locked her office door. "The police are looking for him. Everyone is looking for him. I'm headed home now. Gerald is with me."

Her pause caused him to turn and look at her. He knew what was going on on the other end of the phone. Ella was getting a long dissertation about her spending time with him. Not that he was the bad seed, but when a woman turns down a man's proposal her mother quickly assumes he did something to push her away.

"I'm fine, Mom. I'm in control, and I'm fine. I have to go. I'll call you tomorrow."

Ella exchanged a few pleasantries and sent her love to her father.

As they walked out of the building, she tucked her phone into her purse. "I'm sorry about that."

"Mom isn't too happy about you spending time with me?"

"She doesn't want me to get hurt."

Gerald gritted his teeth, and Ella turned to face him, stopping them from walking to the car.

"Gerald, I'm sorry. I know that…"

"Stop. If we're going to rehash who did what and who said what every day, then this isn't even worth working on."

Ella added, "You're right." She rose on her toes and kissed him gently. "Moving forward."

THE CALL from her mother had put a damper on Ella's mood. Well, the call mixed with her fear about being a victim to someone who was kidnapping women. Admittedly she had a lot on her mind.

They'd chosen to grab Chinese takeout and head home. The silence was their friend tonight, she thought, and a useful step in the right direction. They were comfortable—just as they once had been.

She could never take back the time they'd lost, so she promised herself not to fret over it. They'd have been different people had they gotten married, settled down, and had kids. As it was, she was successful now, and that had been most important.

Ella stirred the noodles in her takeout container with her chopsticks.

"Something on your mind?" Gerald asked, and she lifted her head to see him watching her.

"A lot of things. Sara Crow. Your truck. My mom. That stupid woman whom I represent that keeps wanting more money from her ex-husband."

"Why represent her?"

"Because the firm does. She pays my salary."

"But you don't believe in her cause."

"No, but I believe in Nichole's cause. I have to put up with stupid cases like divorce, petty theft, and parking tickets to get to make an impact for people like Nichole when they need me."

A smile formed on his lips and lit in his eyes. "I hadn't thought of it that way. My family is very grateful to you for helping her out."

"She's a good woman who loves her children and wants the best for them."

"I think they're in good hands now."

"I agree. Your brother is a fortunate man. All of your brothers are lucky. They've married some terrific women."

All of those women would have been her sisters-in-law, she thought, as she gathered noodles and slurped them out of the container. Had all things gone as initially planned, she would have been the first Mrs. Walker. As it was, Gerald was now the last of his brothers to get married, and the last to move from the main house. Had she held him back? Was that all her fault?

"I have to drive up to Atlanta next week. We're picking up two new steers. Would you be interested in going with me?" Gerald eased back in his chair and took a pull from his beer.

"I suppose it would depend on what day."

"I can make it any day. This guy is getting paid handsomely. He'll meet me any time."

Ella set down her chopsticks and picked up her glass of wine as she contemplated his offer. "I suppose I could manage a Friday off."

"Perfect. Why don't I tell him I'll meet him on Sunday morning, and we'll make a weekend of it. We'll take our time and drive up on Friday, spend Saturday in the city, and come back on Sunday."

"Do you remember the last time we spent the weekend in Atlanta?"

The moment she'd asked she'd wished she hadn't. Of course, he remembered.

"I promise not to propose this time," he said before finishing off his beer and carrying the bottle to the recycle bin.

She knew she shouldn't have said anything. In his head, he'd always remember that it was the weekend he'd proposed and was turned down, but she remembered the magic of it—the fancy hotel room, room service, and the white cotton robes. He'd wined her, dined her, and made it the most romantic weekend she'd ever had.

He'd planned out every detail, but to her, it had been spontaneous and beautiful. They'd made love in the king-sized bed, and taken leisurely soaks in the tub built for two. Walks through the city at night had been one of her favorite memories, and ones she went back to most often when things weren't working in her life.

But then, when he'd taken her to dinner, gotten down on one knee and held up the box with the ring in it, she'd panicked.

He'd looked up at her with those dark eyes and asked her to be his wife. He hadn't even gotten the ring out before she'd said no.

No. That word echoed in her head hard enough that it gave her a headache. She'd told the man she loved she wouldn't be his wife. After trying to explain herself, she finally ran out of the restaurant and took a cab back to Macon.

She'd been embarrassed and decided to get on a plane the next day and disappear. She hadn't made it too far when she'd run into Jacob Young, who was well versed in what had happened—of course he was. At the time he'd been Gerald's best friend.

But he got her to open up. The answer she'd given Gerald could have been smoothed over. She'd wanted to focus on her career and not on building a family at the time. It wasn't that she didn't love the man, and she'd never stopped loving him either. It was that the timing was off.

However, she looked like a complete ass when a few months later she ran off and married Jacob. That was a lust-filled marriage and nothing else. He took her mind off Gerald and what could have been. She worked hard, built her career just as she'd wanted to, and at night her mind was pulled away from the what-could-have-beens.

She knew it was never going to last with Jacob. How could it have? She knew his character, and she used him as much as he used her. After all this time, she could admit that now.

Gerald walked to the refrigerator and took out another beer. He opened it and discarded the top.

Ella gathered her containers, closed them, and carried them to the refrigerator. She'd ruined the evening by mentioning the weekend at all.

She set the containers on the shelf and closed the door a little harder than she'd meant to. As she spun back to the table, Gerald reached for her arm and pulled her to him.

"We're not going to do this. You're not going to mention that weekend and then fly through here on a mad rush. Get over it."

"I can't," she admitted, and she could feel the sting of the tears trying to surface.

"It's always going to be there between us. We can either let it ruin what we could have, or we can ignore it. I can ignore it. Can you?"

The tears no longer only threatened, now they fell. "I hurt you."

"Oh, yeah you did. Nearly turned me into an alcoholic."

"Gerald..."

"I'm not kidding. You hurt me more than anyone ever could have, but here I am. Ella, I love you. I'm not going to let you throw away what we should have had—not again."

The tears stalled as his words resonated. *I love you.* He'd said them. He hadn't even had to think about them. He'd just said them.

"What did you say?"

"You heard me. I'm not going to let you throw all of this away."

"No. The other thing."

Gerald's shoulders dropped. "I said I love you."

"You did, didn't you?" Her voice shook as she spoke.

"I've been thinking about saying it, but I didn't think it was right. I guess I decided it was time to tell you. Ella, I never stopped loving you. If I had, maybe even for the slightest moment, I wouldn't be here."

Swiftly she wrapped her arms around his neck. "I love you, too. I do," she mumbled as she pressed her mouth to his. "I won't hurt you again. I promise."

"Don't promise. We're going to hurt each other again, it's inevitable."

"Not like before," she swore. "Never like before."

Gerald lifted her, and she wrapped her legs around his waist as he carried her down the hall to her bedroom. In her heart, she was sure that her promise was true. She never wanted to hurt him again. It was time to accept that future she'd shunned years ago.

erald had stayed at her house, and the next night Ella at his. How quickly something had become a habit.

Ella had managed to take Friday off, with help from Abe reworking her schedule, and seated next to Gerald in his beat up, red pickup, they started for Atlanta with the livestock trailer behind.

She remembered making such trips with Gerald and his brothers years ago. It was part of their routine. Road trips were nothing for the Walkers. Hell, just to get out to their house was a road trip. But the more she made it, the shorter it became.

Ella rested her head on Gerald's shoulder as they cruised down the highway. There was no need for words on a sunny afternoon. Old Johnny Cash songs played on the radio, and the hot wind blew through the cab of the truck. It was as if no time had passed between them, and for that she was grateful.

Gerald Walker loved her, he'd said so. And she loved him, and always had.

Before she'd left that morning, she'd stopped in and had her hair done by his cousin Audrey. Lydia had dropped in and had a cup of coffee while her hair color processed. Gia, just back from their trip to Lucca, brought by a few chocolate samples of a new line she'd be carrying.

She admired the women of the *Bridal Mecca* and their forward-thinking ways.

They were all strong and powerful, and they empowered her, Ella Mills—lawyer, to be all that she could be. Wasn't it funny that she'd missed out on what they had all built together? If she had married Gerald back then, would she have been around them building their empire? Would her career have gone a different direction? Would she have a corner office in Lydia's prestigious strip mall? Maybe she would have helped Lydia with contracts on all of her businesses and properties. She could have written up partnership agreements. Maybe she could have done prenuptial work and fit that in with Pearl's bridal business. Heck, Audrey could probably send her lots of customers. Women in salons always talked about the dirt in their lives. Certainly one or two of them would need a lawyer. Wouldn't it be nice to be the kind of lawyer who chose what they did every day? Ella didn't mind standing up for someone in court, but only when she believed in what she was fighting for. Telling some man he needed to give his ex-wife more money because she needed to live a little more lavishly wasn't the kind of law she wanted to practice. But women like Lydia who were building things, she could do good work for them.

Gerald nudged her. "You're a million miles away," he said as he lifted his arm and draped it over her shoulders while keeping his other hand on the wheel.

"I was just thinking about Lydia, Audrey, Pearl, and Gia."

"Amazing women," he admitted. "By the way, Audrey did a great job on your hair." He ran his fingers through it. "It's beautiful."

"Thank you," she said and could feel the heat rise in her cheeks. "I admire what they've built. I even saw a few of Bethany's flower arrangements in each of their stores."

"All they need is Missy to park her race car in front of the building, and every woman who is part of the Walker family would be accounted for," he offered, including his cousin Jake's wife in the fold.

Yes, she thought, if they'd had gotten married years ago, she'd have been part of that. She wasn't going to share that with him now. No need. That was the bed she'd made and slept in. From here on out, she could do better.

"What in the hell?" Gerald pulled his arm back and placed his other hand on the steering wheel about the time Ella heard the sirens behind them.

"What's going on?"

"I'm getting pulled over. We weren't speeding. The trailer lights are working, and the plate is current. I checked all of that before we left town. I swear to you if Phillip sent them after me, I'll kill him."

She saw the color change in his face, and she wasn't so sure he wasn't serious.

Gerald pulled the truck to the side of the road and put it in park, then killed the engine. And, as if he knew all the following requests, he pulled his license from his wallet and opened the glove compartment to pull out his registration. It was then she saw the gun that he kept there as he quickly closed the door to the compartment before the officers had walked around the truck.

"Afternoon," the first officer said who came to the door. Ella noted the other car that had pulled up and noticed the officer who stood at the passenger door looking in at her. "License and registration."

Gerald handed them over without argument. "What's the cause to pull me over? I wasn't speeding, and my trailer is licensed to my family ranch, the tags are current, and the lights were fine when we left."

"And where were you leaving from?"

"Macon."

"Where are you headed?"

"Just outside Atlanta to pick up two steers for our cattle ranch. I can give you the man's number if you'd like to call him. The meeting is for Sunday morning at eight."

The officer studied his license. "You have a concealed."

"I do, sir. I have a gun in the glove compartment."

"Why?"

"Safety on long drives. I also keep it in case I need to ward off a predator among our cattle. This is a work truck. We use it on the ranch."

"Ma'am," he directed the word to Ella. "Are you here willingly?"

"Yes, sir. I am Ella Mills, and I am dating Mr. Walker. We are going to spend a couple of nights in Atlanta before picking up the steer." She reached for her purse and pulled her wallet out, noticing that the officers were on heightened alert as she did so. She handed him her license. "I am a lawyer in Macon."

The officer nodded slowly. "Do you know why we've pulled him over?"

She was sure this had something to do with the missing women again. God, she wished he'd picked a different truck to use for the drive. But he was stubborn like that.

"No, sir," she lied. "I'd be interested in knowing."

The officer lifted his head and looked Gerald straight in the eye as another police cruiser pulled up in front of the truck blocking any possible exit. "Mr. Walker, we've pulled you over because you're under arrest for the kidnapping and murder of Celeste Cordova."

Fury sparked in Gerald's eyes, but respect for the law drew him back. "Sir, I don't know any Celeste Cordova, and I didn't kidnap or kill anyone. If this is still the same guy, his truck matches mine. That's it."

"Description."

"Yeah, well half of the men in Georgia look like me."

"Fair enough. Let's talk DNA."

Ella felt the blood drain from her head as she was sure she was going to faint right there on the bench seat of Gerald's truck.

The officer to her right opened the door. "Ma'am, please step out of the truck."

She exchanged one last glance with Gerald, and he nodded. "Do what they say. Call Phillip. This is wrong, Ella. You know this is wrong."

In her heart, she did know that. Deep down inside she knew Gerald Walker wasn't capable of hurting anyone. But for some reason the lightheadedness and the spinning in her stomach made her wonder if she was being foolish. Was the man she loved some serial killer?

CHAPTER 18

E lla paced the room they'd put her in. An armed guard stood at the door. The air was stagnant. The muted sounds from beyond the walls were deafening.

Phillip was on his way, and she hadn't seen Gerald since they'd put him in the back of a police car in handcuffs and driven away.

Standing at the dirty window overlooking the less attractive side of Atlanta, Ella heard the door behind her open. When she turned, she saw Phillip walking in and moving right to her.

He pulled her in and then stepped back to assess her. "You're not hurt are you? You're okay?"

"I'm fine. This is all some mistake. Gerald didn't do this. Gerald doesn't have it in him to do this."

Phillip shook his head. "I thought so too. They have DNA."

"What kind of DNA? This is ridiculous," she said as she broke from Phillips hold. "I'll defend him until the end, Phillip. He didn't do this."

"Another woman is missing."

She felt the vile rush of nerves move through her from her stomach to her throat, but she pushed it down. "He didn't do it."

"Five-foot-three, brunette, tattoo on her wrist."

Ella swallowed hard. "Age?"

"Twenty-eight."

"And Celeste Cordova?"

"Five-three, brunette, tattoo, age twenty-six."

"This guy has kind."

He scanned another look over her. "You're five-what?"

"Five-four. Naturally blonde."

"How old?"

"Thirty-one."

Phillip ran his hand over the back of his neck. "Gerald never dated anyone else after you," he said, but the words hit her hard.

"Ever?"

"Not that I can recall. Maybe a date here or there, but he never got into another relationship. C'mon, the man just left his parents' house."

"Yeah, and you had it searched without him there. We could fold this all back on your department you know." The words had come out forceful and mean. And when Phillip turned, she knew she'd gotten her point across.

"I didn't send anyone out there. I'll admit, when I got the call on Abby McCarrey, I walked through his trailer. Who was out there?"

"I figured you'd know. He said someone was out there after that when he'd was detained in town."

Phillip pulled out a chair from around the long table in the center of the room and sat down. "Gerald's DNA was found on the victim."

"He's been with me almost the entire time this week. And I'm sure his brothers will vouch that when he wasn't with me, he was on the ranch."

Phillip nodded. "I have statements from Eric and Russell already."

The door opened, and Phillip was called out of the room. For another hour, Ella sat alone, a can of Coke rested on the table next to a snack pack of crackers that one of the officers had brought in for her.

When Phillip returned his face was long, and his eyes darkened by worry.

He sat down next to Ella and took her hand. "They found the other missing woman. Jennifer Blane."

The name was familiar to her, and she knew it was for Phillip too. "She worked at the coffee shop down the street from the *Bridal Mecca*."

He nodded. "It's getting a little too close to home. Both she and Celeste were sexually assaulted."

"He's stepped up his game."

"Do you know Steven Cross or Kane—" he paused.

"Evans?" She completed his question.

"Yeah, him."

"I know Kane, not Steven. Kane is a ranch hand on the Maguire's ranch. Another ten miles out further than the Walker's."

"Steven owns a small ranch in the opposite direction of town."

"So what do they have to do with this?"

"They drive old beat up red pickups."

"Most of Georgia does."

"They're equal in description to Gerald."

"Again, most of Georgia is."

"Their DNA was found on Jennifer Blane's body."

Ella dropped her head into her hands. "Do you think whoever is doing this is planting DNA?"

"Yeah, that's what I think. Kane did have a date a few weeks back with Celeste Cordova. Coffee date and done, is what I'm told. I have my entire team working on this."

"Gerald is innocent."

Phillip rested his hand on Ella's. "I think he is too. Eric is en route to pay his bail. Russell is meeting up with the man to get the steer. Gerald is going to need you."

"I won't let him down."

IT WAS NEARLY four hours before she saw Gerald again, and another three after that before they were piled into Eric's truck and headed back to Macon in silence.

Ella sat alone in the back seat, and never said a word for the duration of the drive. Eric had taken a few jabs at Gerald, perhaps to feel him out. There was no way anyone in the Walker family thought he'd done anything wrong, but they'd razz him and get him worked up over it as often as they could. That was how brothers worked.

When they returned to Macon, Eric drove straight to Ella's. He jumped out of the truck and pulled open her door, then walked her to her front door while Gerald stewed in the truck.

"Why don't you pack a bag and come back out with us. You don't have to stay with him. He won't be good company. You can stay with Susan and me," he offered.

"I'll be fine, Eric. Thank you for the invitation. Candi has already texted and said she's on her way. She won't let me be alone either."

"Good." He rested his hand on her arm in a sign of comfort. "He's going to be okay. He's pissed. He should be pissed. I know he didn't do this."

"I know it too," she said, looking back at the truck and the man whose shoulders hunched in the seat. "Take care of him. Don't let him go do something stupid."

"He won't. And I know Phillip has given him a hard time, but he won't let anything happen to him either. Phillip will fight for him."

"I can't believe someone did this. Someone set him up."

"People are sick. Anyone who kidnaps and kills—there's a special kind of hell for them."

"You're right. My office will defend him and make sure his name is cleared."

Eric pulled her in and hugged her tightly. "He loves you. He always has. Thanks for being here."

"I wouldn't be anywhere else if your family needed me." It seemed imperative that he understood that.

With a weary smile, Eric walked back to his truck as Ella opened the door.

She watched as Eric pulled away from the curb and Gerald lifted his eyes to meet hers.

CHAPTER 19

S usan had taken the kids into town early that morning, and Eric fumed over breakfast while Gerald nursed a cup of coffee at the breakfast counter.

"I should have had her make us something before she left," Eric said as he shoveled darkened scrambled eggs off the plate.

"Did they leave because I'm some felon?" Gerald bit out the words as his brother slid a plate in front of him.

"I've been shot, and my house burnt to the ground because some lunatic had some manic, lustful episode over one of our cousins. You can't blame any of us for being a little careful."

"You don't trust me."

"I don't trust what's happening to you. And if for one second you think that I have even one inkling that you might have done this then you're an asshole. I'm your brother, and I will always have your back."

At that moment the front door of the house opened and in walked his other brothers, and his cousin Todd.

Russell moved in and took the stool next to Gerald. "Susan go on strike? Who made these eggs?" he asked as he took Gerald's fork and took a bite. "Man, didn't you take the shells out?"

Ben snorted out a laugh. "Thank God my wife makes me breakfast. It's dictated by the two-year-old I now live with, but a bowl of Lucky Charms looks better than this crap."

Dane walked past all of them and straight into the kitchen for a mug, which he promptly filled to the brim with coffee. "You picked a crap week to get arrested and need all this attention. I still have jet lag."

Todd followed his cousin into the kitchen and poured himself a cup of coffee as well. "You're a pansy. Jet lag is a myth."

"My ass," Dane challenged. "Oh, you think you can beat it. You determine when you fly, or when you sleep, and that first day back, you think you've won the challenge. Two days later you can't keep your freaking eyes open."

"I suppose if I ever get the chance even to leave this country for any reason, I'll make those decisions for myself." Todd sipped from his mug and looked up at Gerald. "You look like crap."

"Aren't you full of niceness today," Gerald pushed the plate of burnt eggs toward Russell, who continued to eat them. "I don't need you all out here to babysit me. I'm not going anywhere, as instructed. I don't even have my truck. And Phillip and crew are going through all my personal belongings as we speak. So I'd much rather be left the hell alone."

"Dad is standing guard over Phillip and crew," Russell informed him. "He's talking lawsuit, too, if the name of the ranch and the family get pulled down over all of this."

"It's all bullshit," Gerald picked up his coffee and set it back down. "Each of us has had our own crap to deal with, but this is asinine. I didn't know any of those women. I didn't touch any of those women. And I sure as hell didn't kill any of them. What the hell is an alibi good for if they don't believe it? If I wasn't with Ella when those women were taken and found, then most likely I was with one of you. Hell, I was having a beer with Phillip when he got the call about the first one."

Dane moved to the door when they heard vehicles driving up toward the house. "Dad and Phillip are here."

"Oh great. Someone shoot me if he's here to haul me back."

Gerald said as he spun around to look at the front door as it opened.

Their father walked in without a word, followed by Phillip who promptly took off his hat and ran his fingers over the brim.

"Good morning, gentlemen," he greeted.

"Sure as hell would be if you'd tell them all to let me off my leash and that this nightmare is over," Gerald snarled.

"Not yet. I need to talk to you. Mind stepping outside?" he directed his question to Gerald.

"I don't have anything to say to you that I wouldn't say in front of my family. I have nothing to hide, Smythe."

"Fair enough. Who'd you buy that trailer from?"

"Les Martin. Had never met him before that."

"Where did you find him?"

"Lydia. Who else in this town can match you with a guy who has something if you want it? Maybe you should be asking her to find your man. She knows everyone and what they're doing."

"You can leave Lydia out of this," Phillip's voice grew sharper.

"I'm just saying. I needed a temporary place, and she knew a guy. She arranged the meeting and went with me to meet the guy. He had good things to say about Lydia, because who doesn't?" He made sure to emphasize his feelings about that. "The guy's price was a steal. I paid him in cash. He signed over the title. I pulled it up to my lot of land where it sits right now. Tell me when you tossed all my drawers you put my underwear back where you found it."

Phillip chewed on his bottom lip. "You're a slob. Do you ever clean out your sink after you shave?"

Gerald stood from his stool and Russell was quick to put an arm out to stop his forward motion.

"What the hell does it matter to you?"

"That's where our perpetrator picked up your DNA. Same thing with Steven Cross and Kane Evans. The DNA found on our victims were tiny hairs, just like those you'd have shaved off."

"That's impossible. That would mean he'd had to have been in my trailer."

Phillip nodded. "You said you thought my guys were out here going through your stuff, but I didn't send anyone."

"Don't lie to me in front of my family," he threatened.

"Wouldn't dream of it. We have a few fingerprints we've lifted off of things. I'm sure we're going to find that they are yours and Ella's. Who else have you had out there?"

"Lydia had walked through it with me when I met the guy. Seeing that he'd all but bleached the hell out of it before we got there, I'm going to say Lydia, Ella, myself, oh and you. Those would be the prints you'll lift."

"Steven Cross had a red horse blanket taken from the back of his red pickup. That blanket was found wrapped around Celeste Cordova's body. Your hair is on that blanket."

"I don't know Steven Cross."

"I got that. Stay out here and away from town. Do Ella and Lydia a favor and stay away from them, too, for a few days."

"You don't dictate my life."

Eric moved in to stand between the men. "We'll keep him busy and away from his trailer." He held up his hand when he heard Gerald take the breath to argue. "He's given you all his alibis, so does he get let off a little?"

"When I don't have any more victims, and I have a culprit."

"It doesn't lead to him."

"Does as long as DNA is found there."

"Had he been sleeping in the woman's house and those hairs were on her pillow, fine. You're telling us that the guy responsible for doing this went into his house and collected those hairs. Doesn't that say he's innocent?"

"It says I have DNA confirmation." Phillip said firmly. "I've had my beef with every one of you in this room, and yet I don't wish any harm to any of you," he added.

"Even Gerald? He made moves on your girl," Eric continued.

Gerald shoved his brother. "Are you trying to get me killed?"

"I'm just making sure he doesn't have motive to put you away because he's harboring some feelings over it."

Phillip shook his head. "I got the message loud and clear about what happened between him and Lydia. I want the Walker name cleared as much as you do. And I don't want another dead woman on my hands. If it means I'm an ass to a family that doesn't deserve it, I apologize. I'm here to do my job and do it thoroughly."

"Then you go do your job," Eric said. "We'll keep him out of his truck, his house, and town. Don't let us down."

Phillip put his hat back on his head and pulled it low to his brow. "I wouldn't dream of it."

CHAPTER 20

Ella felt isolated. Wasn't it funny that she was free to go where she wanted to go, talk to anyone she wanted to talk to, but she was the one feeling down about the situation at hand?

Gerald had warned her away from the ranch, so she'd obliged. She'd spent the weekend with Candi, and now she was spending her lunch break wandering the streets, lonely. She wouldn't have had Gerald standing in her office on a Monday mid-day anyway, but she couldn't help but miss him so terribly that she was nearly feeling sick over it.

Phillip was keeping her abreast of everything as it happened. He assured her that Gerald was under the watchful eyes of all his brothers, his parents, and his cousin. She knew he'd turned off his phone just to not be bothered. And she knew she was foolish for feeling so pitiful.

As she came to the end of the street, she watched as Lydia passed by the flower store and Bethany walked out the door. Together they both walked into Pearl's bridal store. Audrey and Gia both walked from their stores as well and entered Pearl's store.

What could all of the Walker women be doing?

Quickly she ducked into the coffee shop, ordered herself a latte, and as she walked out, she saw Susan and her children enter the store as well. Yes, this was a meeting of the greater minds of the Walker family. Would it be presumptuous of her to walk in too?

Perhaps they'd turn her right back to the street. But Ella felt as if she were to be there.

Ella walked to the front of the bridal shop just as Chelsea, Russel's wife walked around the corner with her baby on her hip.

"Oh, Ella. It's nice to see you. I didn't get to talk to you at Ben and Nichole's wedding."

"You're looking well."

"Motherhood will keep you running. Russ took Lucas with him out to fix fence this morning. I'm glad. I needed a little break."

"I'm sure it's tiring. Are you going into Pearl's?"

Chelsea's eyes grew wide. "Yes. Are you?"

"I thought I'd peek my head in," she said as she opened the door for the last of the Walker women to enter, and then she followed her inside.

Sunshine, Pearl's assistant, was wrangling the kids into the break room for lunch. She waved as Ella entered behind Chelsea.

Lunch had been set out in the dressing area, and she had noticed that the sign on the door had been turned to closed. Now she was feeling out of place and considered turning around, but Bethany caught her attention and moved in to hug her.

"It's nice to see you. I didn't know you were coming to lunch."

"Oh," Ella sighed. "I just was down the street and, well, I saw you walk in and thought I'd come to say hi. I didn't know you were all meeting for lunch."

At that moment the door opened again, and Missy, Jake's wife, and Gerald's mother walked through the door. Each of them smiled in greeting, but she didn't miss the looks on their faces, their eyes open wide in surprise that she was there.

"Hey, Ella," Missy said as she passed right by them.

Gerald's mother moved to her and hugged her. "What a nice surprise that you're joining us."

"Oh, I'm not. I just…"

"Of course you should join us," Pearl's voice rang from the doorway. "I should have told you to meet us here anyway."

Pearl took her hand and led her to the room where every woman, a Walker or involved with a Walker man on either side of the family, sat around an ornate tray of finger sandwiches, no doubt put together by Susan.

Every one of them hugged her and greeted her as if she'd never left the graces of the family. The thought crossed her might again, had she married Gerald originally, she would have been the first Mrs. Walker of the generation. Though she and Chelsea might have had to vie for that position, they had both taken different paths before getting involved again. There was some comfort in the fact that she hadn't been the only woman to walk away from a Walker man.

"This is lovely," Ella said as they all began to reach for sandwiches and sip on champagne, which was a staple at the bridal boutique. "Do you do this often?"

Lydia reached in for a sandwich. "We're thinking about having a high tea at the reception hall once a week for the retired community. But it has to be just right. Susan is trying out sandwich recipes," she said, and Ella realized that even among Walker women, Lydia belonged.

"So, Ella, what's going on with Gerald and this serial killer?" Missy asked bluntly, and all eyes turned to her. "C'mon, I'm the only one with enough guts to ask. All the men are tied up trying to keep him out of trouble. What's your take?"

No one argued Missy's question verbally. Instead, all eyes turned to Ella, and she swallowed hard.

"Well, I think it's quite unfortunate. There is no way he could do something like this."

"Agreed," his mother said lifting her glass in salute.

"From what I know, the victims are all similar. He started with the youngest but didn't hurt her. Scared her to death. Enough so that I've heard the family is moving out of the area. He worked his way up from just kidnapping, to battery, to sexual assault. I don't think he meant to kill Sara Crow, but it happened. People like that then get that in their blood and continue with the attacks, and they grow in severity."

"You knew Sara, didn't you?" Bethany asked.

"She worked in my building. I did know her."

"What is he looking for in a victim?"

Ella took a long breath and looked around the room. "Each of them had dark hair," she began and noticed Pearl ease back in her seat. "He started with a teenager and has grown in age by a few years each time. As if he's searching for the right age."

Gia shook her head in disgust. "That's horrible."

"They've all been about five-foot-three," she continued and noticed Bethany's shoulders ease.

Nichole sipped from her glass. "There was something else though. I saw it on the news. One more similarity."

"A tattoo on their wrist," Ella said and watched as Lydia threw her hands up in the air.

"Well, fu..." She stopped herself and looked directly at Gerald's mother who smiled sweetly. Lydia turned over her arm and flashed the infinity symbol, interrupted with a tiny heart on one of the lines freshly inked on her wrist.

Bethany grabbed Lydia's wrist. "When did you get that?"

"Last weekend."

"It's quite personal. Infinity and a heart. You have some dishing to do. Spill."

Lydia shook her head, and her short cap of hair moved with

the motion. "There is nothing to spill. It's a lovely sentiment that means embrace life to me. That's all."

Bethany sized Lydia up and then laughed. "I think that's sweet."

"Yeah, well I'm going to lock myself in my freaking office until that maniac is caught. I fit his profile."

Pearl crossed one leg over the other and rested her bangled wrist on her knee. "He'd have a death wish of his own if he messed with you. Everyone knows you can handle yourself."

"Damn straight," Lydia agreed as she picked up her flute of champagne and drank it down before the alarm on her phone went off. "Well, this was fun. I have a showing for a couple in twenty minutes. I have to get the final touches on my presentation. If you girls do anymore gossiping, you'd better let me in on it. I don't want to be the missing link."

She stood and hurried toward the door.

"Our secretary will take notes," Missy shouted out, and Lydia raised her middle finger to the room filled with laughter that followed her exit.

CHAPTER 21

Ella's head felt light as she walked back to her office. She could never have imagined that she'd have fallen into a lunch with all of the Walker women and have enjoyed herself as much as she had.

Abe had called three times looking for her, as her client had been waiting to go over the new information on getting more money out of her ex-husband. Quite frankly, Ella didn't even care. The woman could wait days if it were up to her.

The thought continued to swirl in her head that she should have her own boutique law firm. She could do the things she wanted to do. Hell, maybe she could even do weddings, it was nothing for someone to get ordained. She could have them sign their prenup and then marry them right off.

Laughing, she stepped off the elevator as her phone rang in her pocket.

Her client zeroed in on her and moved to her quickly, so Ella answered her phone quicker.

"Ella Mills here."

"Gerald Walker here," his voice resonated in her already fuzzy head, and it made her heart rate quicken.

"Well, hello, Mr. Walker. How can I assist you today?" she asked as the woman followed her into her office noticeably irritated.

"Phillip is letting me off my leash just a bit. Come out and stay with me. I want to see you. Touch you. Hold you," he said, and every nerve in her body ignited.

"I'll bring something with me, and I'll be there by six."

"It can't come soon enough. Hey, Mom said she had lunch with you and the girls. She's pleased you're back."

And that was the icing on the cake. "I'll see you at six."

"I'll be here," he said before the call disconnected and she stared into the disgusted face of her client.

GERALD WAS SITTING in one of his lawn chairs when she arrived. He looked more relaxed than he had in weeks, she thought. In his hand, he had a beer, and on a turned over bucket, he had a pail of ice and four more beers cooling. He deserved that, she thought, as she climbed from her car and pulled the bag of groceries out of the back seat.

"You look comfortable," she called to him, and he stood to meet her after setting his open beer on his makeshift table.

"Comfortable. I'm not sure that's the word that describes me, but I'll take it. You brought groceries?" he asked as he reached for the first bag.

"Yes. I thought we could cook dinner, and have something for breakfast. I got you a few things for lunch too."

"Well, aren't you maternal," he noted as he walked back and picked up his beer.

"Just helping out. Do I sense some sarcasm? If you don't want me out here then..."

"What I want is to have this damn thing over. I can't do my work. I can't leave my house. I can't drive my damned truck.

God forbid, I want to go into town to see you, then I'll get arrested."

"You're not charged. Phillip is trying to keep you safe."

"Well, I've had enough of it. Maybe Phillip is the one killing these girls, and he's just pissed off at me because I kissed Lydia and took her home."

She realized that the bucket of beer wasn't to share, and he'd probably already gotten quite a head start on her arrival. He hadn't sounded so angry when he'd called her earlier.

"Are we still going to hash the Lydia thing around? Do you have some unresolved issues about this?" Ella set the second bag of groceries in the empty lawn chair, pulled a beer from the pail, and opened it with the opener he had sitting on the bucket. She took a long hefty swig and wiped her mouth with the back of her hand. She deserved to be good and drunk too if this was what he was going to put her through. Once upon a time she could drink to keep up with him. She sure as hell could do it again.

"You're jealous," he scoffed as he finished the beer he'd been working on then tossed the bottle into a box near the trailer and opened another.

"Right. I'm jealous of a woman who turned you down."

"I could have stayed in her bed. She's the one that asked me to have sex with her. Yet, I still turn out to be the bad guy."

Ella, trying to let the comment pass before she reacted, finished her beer, tossed the empty, and followed Gerald's example by opening another too. "And you think all of this is happening to you because Phillip is mad that she asked you to bed instead of him?"

"He's had a stick up his ass for the Walkers for a long time. He'd always have sided with a Morgan long before a Walker."

"Ah, all I've ever known is him saving your asses. And as for the Morgan in his life, it doesn't look as if she's too interested in him."

Gerald laughed a hearty laugh and drank down half the beer

in his hand. "The point is, she didn't want me at all. She didn't want to have sex with me, even though she said if we had, she wouldn't have regretted it."

"Great."

"She lives to make Phillip miserable."

"Noble job," Ella scoffed as she took another long and satisfying pull of her beer.

"Is that what you enjoy? Making me miserable? Like Lydia and Phillip. Did you enjoy my misery?"

She figured he was drunker than she'd first assessed, but now he was looking for a fight. Well, she'd give him one. She could hold her own, and she'd seen him drunk before. He'd more than likely end up in a corner crying than to attack her physically, so she matched his long pull from his beer, finished hers, and tossed the empty into the box where he'd thrown his before opening another.

"No. I didn't enjoy your misery, and I didn't enjoy mine either. Do you think I turned you down and partied my way out of your life?"

"Sure I do. You partied yourself right into Jacob Young's bed."

The word was emphasized, and the desire to smack him right across the face nearly took over the controls of her body, but she eased back.

"Screw you," she shouted and took another beer from the pail. "You don't know what I was going through right then. I had plans, and I got scared. Have you ever in your life been scared, Gerald Walker? Have you?"

"I'm scared that they're going to throw my ass in jail for something I didn't do."

"Then you understand it."

"No. No, I don't understand. I don't understand breaking the heart of the man you love and running away."

"I don't understand it either," she choked out the words, opened the beer, and drank again. "I don't know what made me tell you no except that I was scared of becoming an adult with adult responsibilities. What if we'd gotten married and gotten pregnant? What if I couldn't finish my degree or the first firm wouldn't take me?"

"You married Jacob."

"Because I was lonely and I knew I'd messed up the best thing in my life by turning you away." Her entire world began to spin, and she argued with him as the sun started to set in the sky. "I've never loved anyone as much as I love you. I know you didn't kill those women, or I'd have turned your ass over just as I would hope you'd turn mine over if I ever did anything that hurt someone—more than a broken heart that is," she shook off the buzz that caused her sentences not to make sense. It had been a lot of years since she'd slammed beers, and she was sure she'd be paying for it.

"I was the best thing in your life?" His words slurred too, and Ella blinked hard to bring him into focus.

"Yes. I messed up. People get scared, and they mess up. Sometimes they mess up really good. I messed up really good," she admitted as the words strung together. "If you want me gone again, I'll leave. I'll take my salad mix, and I'll get out of your life. Forever. And ever," she promised as she pulled from her beer again and let it swim in her head.

"You brought salad mix?"

"Yeah, I need something healthy to go with the Oreos I brought you."

His expression softened, and he smiled from one side of his mouth. "And milk."

"Of course, you ass. You like it that way."

Gerald stumbled toward her and hooked one arm around her waist pulling her against him. "I'm drunk."

"I know."

"So are you now. Lightweight."

She brushed her forehead against his chest. "I am a lightweight. I hate you as much as I love you," she affirmed as she eased back to look at him.

"That's how I like it. I'm not hungry for food. Let's go get naked."

Ella leaned against him again. "My head is spinning."

"You drank too fast."

"I had to catch up. I think I need to eat first."

"You're boring," he joked as he gathered the bag he'd laid down. "I could go for some cookies."

CHAPTER 22

They'd eaten enough to absorb most of the alcohol. They'd gone one more round over sleeping with Lydia and what she really meant to Gerald. And they'd had their first bout of sex right on the floor because they couldn't make it to the bed.

As Ella laid in his bed early the next morning, sure that she wasn't going to make it to work, she contemplated the roller-coaster of emotions that she'd gone through in the past few hours. She and Gerald always argued, and they always ended up right where they were now, entangled in one another's arms confessing their love.

She did love him, too. Like a drug she couldn't get enough of, Gerald Walker was her fix. Only now, she never wanted to take the chance that he wouldn't be there for her.

"Gerald, wake up." She shook him until his eyes fluttered.

He immediately clamped his hand over his face to block out the sunlight. "Christ, what?"

"Wake up."

"I'm awake. What time is it?"

"Six."

He sat up quickly and scrubbed his hands over his face. "Eric hasn't been out here yet to wake me up? Damn, I'm late."

"Wait. I have to talk to you."

"Talk," he said as he picked up the shirt he'd discarded on the floor and pulled it on.

"Marry me, Gerald."

He sat for a moment, his back to her. Nerves stirred with the last bit of alcohol that lingered in Ella's stomach and made her sick. He was going to tell her no. Or worse yet, he wasn't going to say anything.

Finally, Gerald turned to her. "You're going to be late for work."

"Did you hear me?"

Gerald slowly nodded. "Yeah, I heard you."

Ella bit down on her bottom lip so hard she was sure she could taste blood. Pulling the sheet up around her naked body, she fought back the tears that threatened. "Okay then."

Inching off the bed, she searched for her clothes. The tears had broken through now.

She was an idiot to think that would have worked. It was stupid to have said that, especially after they'd tied one on and after the few weeks he'd had. The last thing he needed was her asking him to marry him.

Yanking on the slacks and the blouse she'd worn out to his house, she searched for her pumps. Screw it. She had a closet full of nice shoes and suits. She'd just drive home and put on another one, she decided as she brushed away tears that rolled down her cheeks.

With her blouse buttoned crooked, one shoe and her suit jacket in the crook of her arm, she started out the door.

"Ella. Ella, wait," Gerald called from behind her as she stumbled over the rocky dirt in her bare feet.

He was swifter. Gerald moved in between her and the car door in only his unbuttoned jeans, stopping her from opening it.

"You are the most stubborn woman I have ever met," he claimed as he ran his hand over his messed hair.

"Get out of my way, Gerald."

"Settle down, will ya?" He reached his hand to her face and brushed away the tears that fell. "You're a mess."

"Go to hell," she bit out through gritted teeth.

Gerald laughed. "Perhaps this is how it should have been all along."

Ella caught a glance of herself in the reflection of the window. Her makeup blackened her eyes, and her hair—well there were no words. She was a mess.

"Can I go now? I just want to go."

He smiled, and in the dirt, barefooted and bare chested, Gerald knelt down in front of her.

"You took my glory away once, you don't get to do it again." He reached into the front pocket of his jeans and pulled out a ring—her ring. "Ella Mills, I've loved you since I was a teenager. I've mourned you most of my adult life. I'm better when you're with me. Everything that has been going on in my life would have driven me to the brink of insanity, but all along I've known that in the end you'll be here this time. I was kind of waiting until this all blew over. I wanted to take you away, maybe even Hawaii, and do this on a beach. But, knee in the dirt without my shirt or shoes on, this will work too. Ella, marry me."

Ella covered her mouth with her free hand and let the tears roll down her cheeks. Mascara burned her eyes, but she couldn't stop it now. "Gerald, you saved my ring."

"Of course I did. It's your ring. Made for you. Always for you."

Ella reached out her trembling hand and Gerald took it. "Is this yes?"

She couldn't form the word now. Her throat was clogged with tears. Instead, she nodded until he slid the ring on her finger.

"This time it's forever, Ella. No take backs," he said on a laugh as he stood and gathered her in his arms. "I love you. I promise you so much more than what's before you right now. Your career can come before we have a family. Whatever time you need. I just want you, Ella."

"Shut up," she demanded as she dropped her shoe and jacket to the dirt, rose on her bare toes and kissed the man until she thought the spinning in her head might make her pass out.

She was engaged. She was in love. She was as drunk on happiness as she'd been on the beer.

GERALD FIGURED the proposal in the dirt, half dressed, and Ella with makeup staining her face was appropriate for them. Nothing had ever gone exactly as planned when it came to the two of them, why should this be any different.

He'd never even considered selling the ring he'd had made for her so many years earlier. As far as he'd been concerned, it was always hers.

Holding the woman that would be his wife close to him filled the holes that had surfaced in him over the years. Nothing could take the happiness of the moment away from him, he thought as he heard the sound of tires on gravel racing toward them.

Eric, he figured, finally deciding to come and wake him up, but when the truck came into view over the hill it wasn't Eric's. He was certain the truck was Phillip Smythe's personal truck.

As Phillip skidded to a stop just feet from them, Gerald pulled Ella out of the way and tucked her behind him.

He could already see the fury in Phillip's eyes as he climbed from the truck and swiftly moved to him, his hand balled into a fist that pulled back and cracked Gerald right in the jaw when executed.

Gerald stumbled back, taking Ella with him.

"What in the hell is your..." The words were cut short as Phillip took another swing, this time knocking Gerald to the ground.

The metallic taste of blood filled his mouth as he struggled to get to his feet before Phillip landed another punch. This time though, Ella had stepped in between them, and thankfully Phillip hadn't pushed her out of the way.

Gerald managed to his knee before looking up at Phillip, whose fists were ready to go again.

"You've lost your freaking mind! What in the hell are you doing out here? I didn't invite you, and you're not in uniform, which means your trespassing, so get the hell off my property!" Gerald's voice rose as he did.

"Where's your truck?"

"At the barn where it was towed and Eric told me to leave it."

"It was at Lydia's house all night, you son-of-a-bitch!" Phillip took one more step, and Gerald met that step with his own.

Ella held up her hands and warded them both apart. "You boys are being asses. Now settle down." She turned to Phillip. "Once again, he wasn't anywhere but here. I have been with him all night long. All-night-long," she said as she held up her hand and showed him the ring that sparkled on it. "Enough said. He's not sleeping with Lydia or anyone else for that matter. Now take your jealous heart and..."

"She's gone, asshole," Phillip spat out the words. "Your truck is in the driveway and Lydia is gone and so is her car."

Gerald wiped the blood from his mouth with the back of his hand. "I can't even imagine what you're trying to tell me. I told you. My truck is at the barn. Head down and check for yourself and ask Eric."

"I did," Phillip admitted as they heard more vehicles coming up over the hill.

Just as Phillip had done, Eric and Russell both skidded to a stop inches from one another and jumped out of their trucks.

"Damnit, Phillip, I told you I'd talk to him," Eric said as he hurried to put himself between them. "Did you punch him? You've lost your mind."

"That's what I told him," Gerald interjected.

Phillip loosened his fists and then balled them back up. "His truck isn't at the barn, it's at Lydia's house."

Eric turned too Gerald. "He's right. It's not at the barn."

Gerald moved to his brother, and again Ella eased him back. "What the hell do you mean it's not there? I left it there."

"You did," Eric agreed. "But this morning when Phillip got there, I looked. It's not there."

Gerald could feel the blood drain from his head. "I don't know what's going on. I didn't drive it anywhere. I haven't seen Lydia for a few days."

Phillip ran his hand over the top of his head. "All I know is your truck is in her driveway, and her car is not. I went to the door and she didn't answer. I went to the back door and it was unlocked, and she never does that. I went in and..."

Ella moved to Phillip and took his hand. "Phillip, what happened?"

Gerald saw the tears in Phillip's eyes. This man who had seen the best and worst of mankind had seen something to terrify him. Now he moved to Phillip.

"What happened?"

"Her house is torn up. Like there was a struggle. The bed is a mess. Chairs are overturned. Knives in the kitchen are..." He couldn't go on.

Gerald's first reaction was to condemn the man who usually held it together. Why had Phillip driven forty-five minutes to punch him in the face instead of calling in his own people to search for Lydia? But when Ella turned to him, her eyes filled with tears, he understood it.

Phillip was just a man in love with a woman. All sense was gone when that woman was gone.

CHAPTER 23

Gerald and Russell had managed to get Phillip to sit down, and Ella made him a cup of coffee. Eric put in a call to the police station.

His face was long when he'd turned around from his truck and walked back to where the rest of them fussed over Phillip.

"I'm going to drive you back into town," Eric told Phillip. "They have deputies already at Lydia's. A neighbor had called in strange activity, including Gerald's truck in the yard." He ran his hand over his chin and took in a breath. "Steven Cross and Kane Evans' trucks were both reported stolen this morning. Both have been found in the driveways of two other women, who are also missing."

Ella put her hand to her stomach. "I think I'm going to be sick."

Gerald reached for her and touched her arm.

"What can we do?" he asked Eric.

"I'm going to take Phillip into town. You two follow me out there. Russell, you make sure Chelsea, Susan, and the kids are safe at Mom and Dad's. Pearl already texted and said that she and Audrey were headed to the *Bridal Mecca*.

She is going to let the police in to go through the reception hall. She said Lydia had a meeting there after lunch yesterday."

Ella nodded. "She said she was showing someone the venue."

"Phillip, this is personal now. We all are in. You got it?"

Phillip nodded. "I will kill the son-of-a-bitch that hurts her," he ordered.

Gerald nodded. "We will all back you up."

ELLA HELD on to the inside of the door of her BMW as Gerald sped down the dirt road toward town.

"You killing us both isn't going to help Lydia," she shouted as he hit a rut and the car bounced her around.

"I'm with Phillip. I'll kill the SOB with my own bare hands if I have to."

"Lydia is strong. She's going to be okay."

"Yeah, I'm sure the other women thought they were going to be okay too. Goddamnit!" He slapped his steering wheel. "Why didn't Phillip go right after them? I mean, hell, he had enough time to drive out and punch me in the fricking face?" He rubbed his jaw where Phillip had landed the first punch.

"He's distraught. I see it all the time. People don't do what they're trained to do when it becomes personal."

"He sure as hell should have acted on it."

She reached for Gerald's hand. "He knew his team was on it. For one moment he could mourn what had happened. He's going to find her. We're going to find her," she promised.

Gerald squeezed her hand, but it reached right into her heart. She wasn't going to rehash the Gerald and Lydia thing again. She'd been put in her place enough times, she decided. But how personal was this, she wondered? Did his feelings go deeper than friendship?

The vile thought made her even sicker. She shouldn't even be thinking like that. This wasn't about her. This was about Lydia who could be going through hell at that very moment.

Tears quickly came, and they poured down her cheeks.

"Why are you crying?" Gerald asked as he shifted a look from the road to her and back again.

"I'm worried. Each time that guy has stepped up his game. And it was as if Lydia knew she was prime for him."

"What the hell does that mean?"

"At lunch yesterday, we were talking about it. She's the right height, right hair, and she has a tattoo on her wrist."

Gerald shifted another glance her way. "What tattoo? She doesn't have a tattoo."

"She does now. It's new. An infinity symbol with a single little heart. It's on her wrist."

"Damnit. It's like she led herself right to this guy."

The tears dried quickly, and Ella brushed away the ones that lingered on her cheeks. "You think she set herself up for this? You're crazy. Lydia wouldn't do anything like this on purpose."

"You think I mean on purpose? God, what's wrong with you?"

And with that, the tears were back. What was wrong with her? Jealousy weirdly surged through her.

Gerald drove straight into town and directly to the police station. Eric must have known a short cut because he and Phillip had pulled in right before them.

Gerald's cousin Jake was already standing at the door. "Any more news?"

"No. But we're going to kill him," Gerald grumbled through gritted teeth. "He thinks he's messing with weak girls, well he messed with the wrong one."

Tyson Morgan, Lydia's brother, and Pearl's husband sped into the parking lot and jumped from his truck. "I'm going to kill whoever did this."

Ella felt compelled to reach for him. "Lydia will kill him first. You have to believe that."

"Oh, I do. I've seen her take down six-foot men." He lifted his eyes to Phillip. "What's the plan?"

"Um. We have to get our information. See what they found." His voice shook as he turned from them and walked into the station.

Tyson's cheeks filled with color. "What in the hell is wrong with him? He should have the entire state looking for her. What a pansy little…"

"He's beside himself," Ella confirmed. "They're moving already. Whoever did this took two other women as far as we know. The two other men, besides Gerald, who were targeted for their trucks and matching descriptions, had their trucks stolen last night and the trucks were found at the houses of the other missing women."

Tyson lifted his stare to Gerald. "Is this because of you? Is this because of you and Lydia at Ben's wedding?"

"Nothing happened between Lydia and me at Ben's wedding."

"Social media said otherwise. I saw the kiss you were taking in on the street. I know you spent the night at her house."

Gerald's shoulders pushed back, and he took one step toward Tyson. "Then you know how it played out too. Your sister isn't stupid, and she doesn't take unnecessary chances. So she took a night off, and I made sure she was okay. End of story."

"And now some maniac with your truck has her."

"And we're going to find her and the other women. This isn't about me now. It's about whoever devised this sick and twisted plan."

Phillip stood just beyond them now, his uniform on, his hat low on his brow, and his face stern. "Les Martin. That would be our sick and twisted bastard."

"Who the hell is Les Martin?" Tyson asked.

Gerald winced at the name. "The man I bought the trailer from. Lydia introduced us."

Phillip walked toward them. Whatever time he'd spent inside

had brought back the serious-minded Phillip, and from the look of him, he was ready to go after Lydia.

"Les Martin is a registered sex offender from Oklahoma. Abby McCarrey just identified him from a picture. One of our officers is there with her now. Records show that he sold you the trailer and each of the other men their trucks. He had keys for everything."

"Not my truck," Gerald offered. "I have the only keys to my truck."

"Did you have one in your trailer?"

"The only spare, yes."

Phillip clucked his tongue. "And he had a key to your trailer."

"Son-of-a-bitch!"

"Athens police are starting an in-depth search of the area since his other victims end up there. We've traced his ex-wife to Athens, so it's a lead."

Gerald rubbed his jaw again. "He's making a point to her?"

"Maybe. They're headed to her now. At this point, he's getting sloppy. Usually, they want the glory of getting caught."

"But he has Lydia. Sloppy isn't what we need. We need Lydia back."

"And we'll get her," Phillip promised. "You're all witnesses to this. If I get my hands on the man, and he's done anything to Lydia or harmed her in any way, this badge comes off. I'll serve justice myself."

Tyson reached out his hand to shake Phillip's. "We'll have your back. Let's go."

CHAPTER 24

E lla's phone blew up with text messages from the girls at
the *Bridal Mecca* and Abe at her office.

Audrey remembered the man who had sold Gerald
the trailer. He'd been a walk-in at the salon on three different
occasions. She'd taken him one time, and he had creeped her out.
He'd come in one evening when Nichole was closing up, but all
she had recalled was that the boys were there too and they were
so wild since she'd taken on an extra client, she hadn't paid too
much mind to the man. One of the other stylists remembered
him quite well.

He's not a fan of blondes, Audrey's text read. *He told her so, and it
made her hurry and get him out of the chair.*

Pearl had never seen the man. Sunshine, Phillip's niece who
worked for her, remembered seeing him walking past the
window slowly. However, he'd never gone into the store.

Bethany was thrilled to have missed out on all the action. She
figured the few times he'd been around the *Bridal Mecca* she must
have been gone, or redheads were not his thing. *Besides*, she'd
texted the group, *I've already dealt with one crazy man who thought I
was my mother—his ex-lover. I'm over crazy.*

Gia was particularly spooked and had even closed her shop and locked herself in Pearl's back room for the day.

I remember him, she texted. *He came into the store a week ago. Walked around for a long time and asked a million questions about Italy, and then about me. He liked my hair. Thought I looked nice in my apron. Then asked if I had a tattoo.*

Ella read the text to Gerald who let out a disgusted grunt. "He's sick."

"That's obvious."

Abe had texted words of encouragement but did let her know that the partners were not very pleased with her disappearance or her lack of focus that past few weeks.

Gerald reached for her hand. "What does that mean for you?"

She shrugged. "I've been having second thoughts about it. Honestly, even though I like to see justice, I like working on contracts and helping people with wills and planning. I don't want to keep fighting a man for more money for his spoiled ex-wife. That's not why I got into law."

"You've given this a lot of thought."

"Not enough. But it looks like I need to give it more."

When Gerald's phone rang, he pulled it from his pocket, keeping one hand on the steering wheel. "Yeah?"

She watched as he took in the information that was being spoken on the other end. Then he took a sharp right off the highway.

"Where are we going?"

"Back," he said as he tossed her his phone. "They found one of the women that were missing in Lydia's crawl space under her house."

Ella swallowed the fear that stuck in her throat? "Dead?"

As Gerald turned the car back toward the highway, he shook his head. "No. Beaten up. Dehydrated. In and out of consciousness, but they said she might be sleep deprived. They're taking her to the hospital and hoping she can give them some information."

"So why are we going back?"

"Phillip seems to think he kept all the girls local because his ex-wife just showed up in Macon at the police station."

"She knows something," Ella said. "Maybe he reached out to her, or most certainly is trying to get into her head."

Gerald nodded. "I can't believe I've talked to the man. I live in his property."

"Your property. You bought it."

"I'm never staying in it again. What if he did this to women in it? I might send it over a cliff."

Ella gripped the handle above the passenger door as Gerald weaved in and out of traffic. "You're not sending it over a cliff. If you get rid of it, where will you live?"

"I don't care. I'll pitch a tent. This is not important right now. What's important is Lydia."

But it was important. For the next half hour, keeping him somewhat focused so he didn't kill them racing back to Macon made it very important.

"Why don't you move in with me, until you get situated. We are engaged, after all." She felt the need to remind him as she glanced at her finger and the ring shimmered there.

Gerald let out a long breath, his shoulders eased, and so did the speed of the car. "We certainly are," he said reaching for her hand.

"She's going to be okay," Ella promised. "Lydia will be okay."

"In my heart, I know that. I just can't wrap my head around it."

GERALD SPED THROUGH TOWN, only this time he headed right to Lydia's house which was flocked with police.

Phillip swiftly moved from the front door when he saw them pull up, and headed right to them.

"You're no help here. Why don't you find something to do," Phillip suggested, his voice full of authority and not that of the whimpering man he'd been earlier that morning.

"Are you kidding me?" Gerald stepped forward. "I was halfway to Athens when I got your call. You fill me in, or I return the favor of the punch you gave me this morning."

Phillip placed his finger against the brim of his hat and tipped it back slightly. "Sylvia Martin walked into the station this morning and said she figured we'd be looking for her. She said her ex-husband had been calling her every day for the past few weeks, threatening her." Phillip took his cell phone out of his pocket, swiped his finger over the screen, and then held it up for Gerald and Ella to see the picture he'd pulled up.

"She looks just like his victims," Gerald pointed out.

Phillip nodded. "She freakishly looks like Lydia."

Ella gripped Gerald's arm. "Maybe he won't hurt her then. Maybe he's mixed up."

Gerald looked down at her. "You think? Serial killer. He's mixed up."

"I mean, if he kept reaching out to his ex-wife, then maybe he will hold on to Lydia."

Phillip tucked his phone back into his pocket. "Olivia Kent was the woman found in Lydia's crawl space. She didn't know how long she'd been there, but she figured at least overnight since it had gotten so dark."

"Could she identify Les Martin?"

"Certainly did. He hasn't done anything to conceal who he is. She was assaulted, sexually, and beaten. It seems as if he's swapping up. Each woman looks more like his ex."

Ella loosened the grip on Gerald's arm. "There were three trucks parked at three different houses?"

"Hannah Welch is still missing. Kane Evans' truck was parked there."

"Does he know Hannah Welch?"

Phillip shook his head. "Never met her before. Steven Cross' truck was found at Olivia's house," he offered the information just as another deputy moved in behind him and directed his attention away from Gerald and Ella.

A moment later he turned back, adjusting his hat low on his brow again. "I'm headed to Olivia Kent's house. They just found Hannah Welch."

Phillip started toward his car as Gerald grabbed his arm to stop him. "He's just moving them from one place to the next."

"Seems that way."

He let Phillip go and then hurried back to Ella's car. "Get in."

"Where are we going? Olivia Kent's house?"

He shook his head as he threw the car into reverse and sped away in the opposite direction. "He's moving these women from one house to the next. Lydia is in Athens."

"How do you know that?"

"He's taking her to Sylvia's house, but Sylvia is here."

"You're scaring me," she said with her voice jumping as she fought to get on her seatbelt.

"It's scaring me too, because the only reason you'd take a replacement back home was if you were going to replace someone, right?"

"You think he's taking Lydia to Sylvia's house, and then planned to kill Sylvia?"

"I think so. But Sylvia isn't there."

"He might turn that all around then."

"Yeah. See, I don't need a badge to figure this out. Phillip should be miles ahead of me, and he's dinking around in town."

"He's doing what he's trained to do."

Gerald picked up speed as he merged onto the highway. "And I'm doing what I'm trained to do—protect my family."

The flash of anger mixed with jealousy flashed across Ella's face. Gerald reached for her hand and squeezed it.

"I'm not in love with Lydia. I'm in love with you, but she's family."

She nodded. "I know. It's all hard to take. She's my friend, and I don't want anything to happen to her."

"Exactly. We need her back in one piece so she can recover by kicking Phillip's ass since he won't be the one to find her."

Ella chuckled. "How do you know where we're going?"

"I don't. You need to get on the phone to your office and have them look up the records. You guys have that power, right?"

"It could be public record."

"Then it should be easy."

CHAPTER 25

Ella put in the call to Abe, who was willing to help and came back quickly with the information, but let her know that things in the office were tense in her absence.

"I will call them as soon as we get back to Macon. Right now I have to do this."

"I get it," Abe whispered into the phone. "If this doesn't work out, and you go to another firm, take me with you."

Ella wrote down the address and plugged it into the map app on her phone. They were set with directions.

"You're not going to help Lydia if you get pulled over and arrested for speeding," she warned Gerald as he darted in and out of traffic.

"We have a timeline."

"Don't you think they have police already mobilized?"

He clucked his tongue. "I'm still going to be there."

Ella tried to relax, but she found it hard to do going twenty miles an hour over the speed limit.

What would happen if they didn't get there in time? Or what if he hadn't taken Lydia to Sylvia's house? Serial killers liked to play mind games, and this could be just that kind of game.

She thought about the picture Phillip had shown them of Sylvia. She was a match for Lydia. Had Lydia only been on the radar since she'd gotten the tattoo? And what did the tattoo mean, she wondered as her phone gave the direction to exit the highway.

"What made Lydia hate Phillip so much?" she asked as Gerald rolled through a stop sign.

"I don't know. I never thought much of Phillip myself until the past few years. Perhaps it was because he's the law and I'm not."

"But you're not a trouble maker, so why worry about the law?"

"It just seems to get in our way, as Walkers. Never provoked, but for some reason trouble finds us."

"Is it the same for the Morgans too? I mean, your families were never friendly."

"That changed a lot when it came to light that Eric is a Morgan. Tyson's mom is Eric's mom. And now Tyson is married to a Walker too. Talk about weaving a new web."

Ella remembered hearing all of the gossip surrounding Eric's lineage and many of the run-ins the Walkers had where Phillip was involved. She supposed it was right that she returned to her hometown. The news always followed her, or she'd sought it out. She hadn't wanted to miss anything in Gerald's life, that was obvious.

Ella's phone gave another set of directions toward Sylvia's house. Twenty minutes later they pulled up in front of a small house, shutters falling away from the windows, the grass not green but brown, and paint chipping from the front door.

Police cars and an ambulance clogged the street. Gerald pushed open the car door, leaving the engine running, and ran toward the barricade of yellow tape.

Ella ran after him, but two officers stepped in front of him, blocking his forward motion.

"This is a crime scene. No one goes in," the officer directed with his arms extended.

Ella heard the words, and nausea that rolled through her had her falling to her knees in the street. One of the officers ran to her.

"Let me get you some medical help," he offered.

"I'm fine. I'm fine," she said through tears that had rolled down her cheeks and clogged her throat. "I just need a minute."

Gerald's hand was on her back, and a moment later his arms were wrapped around her as he too knelt on the ground next to her.

Crime scene. The words were accentuated by the gurney that rolled from the front door, a black bag holding what she could only assume was a body.

Now, instead of kneeling, she sat flat on the ground and let the flood of tears loose. There was no reason to assume that the body they had just carried out of the house wasn't that of Lydia Morgan. The man was a killer, and he had taken their friend and disposed of her just as he had the others.

They were too late. They'd wasted too much time. That bastard had killed her.

"It's okay," Gerald whispered in her ear as she felt her body shake and she couldn't stop. "It's okay."

"It's not okay," she wept against him knowing his words were as much an automatic response as her tears, but she knew he didn't even believe them.

Sirens blared behind them and when she looked up another car had sped up, and Phillip jumped from the passenger seat and ran past them into the house.

Gerald stood. "He had to have been right behind us the entire way up here." He moved to one of the officers who had held him back. "I need to know what's going on."

"This is an investigation. You'll hear about it on the news."

Ella watched as his hands balled into fists at his side. Gathering all of her strength, she stood and moved to him now, hoping that her touch would calm him as his had calmed her.

"Gerald, back up. They have to do their job. Phillip will talk to us. Phillip will…"

She stopped. The whole world seemed to stop in that very moment as Phillip slowly stepped out of the house with his arm protectively wrapped around a bloody and beaten Lydia.

GERALD'S fisted hands fell open as he saw Lydia in the doorway of the house. Her short cap of hair was crusted with blood, her right eye swollen shut, and a large cut was fresh on her left cheek. She favored her right arm as Phillip held on to her and helped her down the two crumbled steps of the front porch.

Gerald made another lunge for the police tape, but the officers held him back, just as before, until Phillip nodded for him to cross and they let him go.

His heart raced in his chest as he ran up the walk. With an arm around Lydia, he helped Phillip guide her to the ambulance that waited for her. Her head rested on Gerald's shoulder, and he was aware that his shirt was now covered in Lydia's blood. The blood that bastard had drawn from her.

But who had they taken from the house, he wondered as they neared the ambulance while Phillip softly spoke words of encouragement to Lydia.

The paramedics helped her onto a gurney that waited for her, and immediately they tended to her cheek, and the gash on her head, which Gerald realized was what had been the source of blood on his shirt.

"She needs to go to the hospital," Phillip said, and Lydia retorted with a growl.

"Let them stick a bandage on me, and I'll be fine. I want to go home. Do you hear me?" Her voice rose, and she looked directly at Gerald. "I want to go home. Just take me home."

"Lydia, you need to go…"

"Shut up," she shouted, cutting off Phillips demands. "I want to go home. Gerald will take me home."

Phillip shifted a stern look his direction, and he took it as his opportunity to talk some sense into Lydia.

"Why don't I go with you to the hospital? Let's let them look you over and then I'll take you home."

She nodded, keeping her eyes averted from Phillip's.

"Let them tend to you a minute, and I'll let Ella know."

He walked back toward Ella and Phillip followed. "Don't you dare let her leave that hospital without them clearing her," Phillip demanded before he grabbed Gerald's shoulder and turned him around. "Don't you let anything else happen to her."

"I wouldn't dream of it. What happened in there?"

Phillip ran his hand over his hair. "I'm still getting details." He swallowed hard and wiped the back of his hand over his eyes. "She killed him. Somehow she killed the bastard. I don't have all the details yet."

"That'a girl," Gerald whispered, proud that Lydia had survived and done what needed to be done.

A smile formed on Phillip's lips and he chuckled as he wiped away more tears. "She killed the son-of-a-bitch."

"Did you have doubts?"

"Yes. I thought I lost her, but she hates me as much as she always has. So that much remains, but when she saw me, she held on to me."

"She needs to process it."

"She hates me," he joked and took a long breath. "Take care of her. Take her home with you. Her house isn't ready to go back to, and I don't want her spending time with her grandfather. Maybe with Tyson and Pearl, but not her grandfather."

"I'll take care of her."

"I'll be here for hours, maybe days."

"She's safe."

Gerald was sure Phillip wanted her to stay with him and let him nurse her back, but that wasn't an option.

"Keep her that way."

Gerald rested a hand on Phillip's shoulder. "I'll take care of her. I promise."

CHAPTER 26

Ella sat in the waiting room of the emergency department. It had been nearly three hours, and she hadn't had any news on Lydia nor seen Gerald.

Tyson had arrived nearly two hours earlier and disappeared to be with his sister, but still, Gerald hadn't come out to make sure she was okay or give her any information.

She'd eaten an old Twix bar and drank four cups of coffee. The last thing she could tolerate was sitting any longer.

Maybe she'd go for a walk around the building. Would Gerald even know she was missing? She could let the front desk know, she decided. They could pass on the message, after all, she was his ride home.

As she approached the desk, Gerald emerged from the back with Tyson. His eyes were dark and dried blood covered his shirt.

"How is she?" Ella asked, and Gerald looked up at her as if he'd forgotten she'd been sitting in the waiting room for hours.

"Ella," he whispered as he walked to her and pulled her into an embrace that had her knees shaking.

"You're scaring me. Is she okay?"

He pulled back and smiled through weary eyes. "She's okay. He got in quite a few licks. Her clavicle is broken, and a few ribs. They want to keep her overnight because she has a massive concussion from being slammed into a wall."

Ella lifted her hand to her mouth and covered it. "She's brave."

"Always. I'm going to stay here with her, all night," he told her before exchanging glances with Tyson. "He's going to give you a ride home."

Ella looked at Tyson. "Why aren't you staying with your sister?"

"She doesn't want me to. You're right, she's very brave, but she's as stubborn as they come. She needs some time to process what happened to her without her big brother looking over her. I'm going to get home and help Pearl get the house in order so I can take care of her in our home. My grandfather will turn this on her in some way, and she doesn't need that. Her mom is a mess, and I don't want that to feed her either. She needs to be pampered and taken care of, and that's what Pearl and I are going to do. But right now the only person she seems to be taking to is Gerald. So he's going to stay."

"Okay." Ella heard her voice crack as she spoke.

"Why don't I walk to you out to his truck while he says goodbye to Lydia?" Gerald offered and wrapped an arm around her waist as he began to lead her from the building.

"Why don't I stay too? I'm fine in the lobby," she offered as the doors opened automatically as they walked through. "It's really no problem."

"That's not what I gather from your conversations with Abe. It sounds like you have your own problems back home too."

She hadn't even considered the issues she had. Nothing much had mattered once Lydia had been taken.

When they reached Tyson's truck, she turned to him. "I just don't understand why it's you that has to stay."

"She's open to me."

"She loves you," Ella said, and quickly realized she hadn't meant to.

"Like a brother," Gerald added. "She's tight-lipped about what happened. Three different officers have been in to talk to her, and she's not ready to discuss it yet. I'm going to see if I can get her to open up to me."

"What did he do to her?" Ella asked and then shook her head. She didn't want to know, she realized. "When will you be home?"

"Tomorrow. I'll keep in touch with you. Keep my side of the bed warm. Remember I live with you now. There's no way in hell I'll go back to my place."

Ella wrapped her arms around his neck and rested her head on his chest. "Forever, right? I mean you're not rethinking this morning are you?"

"Only that you deserved a better proposal." He kissed the top of her head and eased back. "I love you, Ella. This is a horrible thing that has happened, and somehow I got thrown into the middle of it for a lot of different reasons. But every step of the way, you had my back. You defended my honor, even when I wasn't sure you believed it. Why would I ever want anyone else?"

"Promise?"

"I promise."

Tyson cleared his throat as a signal that he was there. He then climbed into the truck and started the engine.

"I'll call you in a bit. Get things settled at the office. I'll be home tomorrow."

Ella gently kissed him before climbing into Tyson's truck. She waved as they drove away, her heart breaking for Lydia and what she'd gone through, and for herself as she watched the man she loved enter the hospital to take care of another woman.

. . .

LYDIA ROLLED her head to see him walk back in the door. He knew she wanted to sit up more, but the pain from her ribs wouldn't allow it.

"Pain meds still working?" he asked as he pulled a chair next to her bed and sat down.

"Yes. I want to go home."

"And you know they'll let you tomorrow. Be calm."

She reached her hand toward him, and he held it in his. "Is Tyson mad?"

"I think he understands. You're not one to like to be fussed over. Well, not like this."

"I have events that need attention. I have clients to book. I have…"

"Shhhh," he said standing from the chair and easing himself onto her bed next to her. "Todd was going to look in on the hall for you. Pearl and Gia and Bethany and Audrey, they all have your back too. You need to take care of you."

Lydia maneuvered until she was resting in his arms, her head against his chest. "He wanted to kill me," she said softly against his shirt. "When the sun came up this morning I was surprised. Genuinely surprised."

"Phillip knew you wouldn't let him hurt you."

"He did hurt me. I'll never get over what happened to me."

"But he knew you'd survive. That's the kind of girl you are."

"A statistic is what I am," she said, and Gerald winced. He wasn't sure how long it would take until she could say the word aloud, but the thought made him sick.

"You're more than that, and you always will be."

Lydia linked fingers with him. "I need to apologize to Phillip."

"He doesn't care. He wants you to be okay, and go on hating him like you always do."

She chuckled and then arched at the pain it caused. "It gets me through my days," she humored, and now he chuckled. "Is Ella mad that you're staying here?"

"I want to say no. She understands. But, yeah, I think it hurts."

"You should have left me and gone with her. I'd have been mad too."

"She was willing to sit in the waiting room all night."

"She was?"

Gerald nodded and brushed a stray hair from Lydia's forehead. "When people love one another they forgive, and they work their way through it. If she's still mad tomorrow, I'll make sure we work our way through it. You can't get married and not trust, right?"

"You're getting married? You're going to ask her to marry you?"

"It kind of happened this morning, very badly," he laughed thinking about it. "She deserves a better proposal, so I'll have to think that over."

"I could help you."

Gerald shifted to look down at her. "What could we do?"

"I'll think on it," she said cozying back up to him. "She's lucky, Gerald. You're a good catch."

"Do you think so?"

"Yeah. I do. You're just not my type."

"What is your type?"

Lydia sighed. "Let's not talk about it."

They were silent for a long time, long enough Gerald wasn't so sure they both hadn't fallen asleep.

"I'm going to leave town for a little bit when I'm healed," Lydia finally broke the silence.

"Where are you going to go?" Gerald whispered against her hair.

"My mom always wanted to go to Hawaii. I think maybe I'll take her, but I'm going to stay there for a while."

"What about your businesses?"

She turned so that she could look up at him. "I'm going to ask Bethany and Todd to help me there. Todd is always offering to help if I need it. Well, now I need it. And it sounds like they're already stepping up. That's how you Walkers work. You help anyone who needs it."

The compliment made him smile. "That sounds good. How long are you thinking you're going to be gone?"

"Until I can move past this. But how long do you think it takes to move past a man drugging you, beating you, threatening you, and..."

She grew silent again. "You'll find out I guess. You're not the kind to let this ruin your life. You'll survive it."

"So you keep saying. Gerald, for the first time in my life I think I'm truly broken."

"But because of you, he will never hurt another person."

"He did enough damage. Entire families will never heal. You won't even go back to your house. Gerald, I'm so sorry I introduced you to him."

"No, no. You could never have known." Again, he kissed the top of her head. "Take the time you need to heal. We're all here for you. Don't you ever, for one minute, think that you're not loved or worthy. Don't think that this defines who you are for the rest of your life. Every Walker I know loves you. And there are plenty of us to go around, so you'll never be alone. And even if you don't want to hear it, Phillip is there for you too."

He expected an argument. Instead, Lydia settled in close to him again, and this time she fell asleep.

CHAPTER 27

Tyson hadn't said much to her on the ride home. He'd made phone calls and plans for his sister. Ella called Nichole, who was setting up a dinner train for Lydia and put her name on the list.

Tyson had Pearl taking down a million notes, and Ella couldn't help but wonder if his wife was doing whatever he asked just to keep him calm. How did anyone see their sister, looking like Lydia had, and not have it shake them to the core?

She decided no one did. Tyson Morgan was trying everything in his power to keep himself calm. The truth was, she was sure he'd like to do something more physical to get his anger out. She knew she would.

There wasn't even an opportunity to make small talk. What would they talk about? The weather? Town gossip? A new fence that kept the Morgans and the Walkers separate? How about the fact that Ella's stomach churned at the very thought of Gerald spending the night with Lydia?

It was stupid to worry. It wasn't as if he were sleeping in Lydia's bed at home. He was going to be uncomfortable in a hospital chair all night. And indeed the best thing that could come out of it was that Lydia might talk to him and give him the answers everyone needed. But deep down inside it still twisted her up.

"How's the lawyer thing going?" Tyson finally asked her a question as if he'd run out of commands to give his wife.

"It's okay. I want to go a different way with it, but we'll see."

"What's a different way?"

"Something private. Not in a big firm like I am now. I want to do things like contracts and wills. That kind of thing. I'm finding that I don't much enjoy chasing down ex-husbands, who paid their part, and asking for more because they ex-wives are greedy."

"That sounds as if that might be a little recent."

Ella laughed as she watched the endless fields pass outside the window. "It is. It's not why I became a lawyer. I wanted to help people, but not like that."

"Lydia uses contracts and lawyers all the time. You should talk to her. She could probably use one in all her business dealings. You know there is a small office in the *Bridal Mecca* that doesn't hold a tenant, but a private lawyer might just fit the bill."

That twisting in her gut became lighter. "Do you think so?"

"Yeah. Think it's worth talking to Lydia about when she's ready to talk."

And then the twisting was back. "I'm not sure Lydia would want to work with me. I don't know how that's all going to play out."

"You're worried about her and Gerald?"

Ella lifted her eyes to catch his glance. "I'm that transparent?"

Tyson shrugged. "I see you have a ring on."

Ella looked down at her hand and twisted the diamond solitaire on her finger. "This morning. I proposed to him, and he came back with my ring, the one he gave me before. That almost makes it sound romantic," she said on a laugh.

"It wasn't?"

"No. Not at all. We were hungover and late for work. It was a mess of a situation, and then Phillip showed up." She let out a breath. "He came right at Gerald and punched him in the jaw. It was if he'd gone crazy."

"Was that after he found out Lydia had been taken?"

"Yes."

Tyson gripped the steering wheel. "I don't know what to think of him. It's obvious my sister doesn't want anything to do with him, but he doesn't get the picture."

"Why does she hate him so much?"

Tyson shifted in his seat. "Sometimes romances don't rekindle, like yours and Gerald's. Sometimes they just go bad. Unfortunately, when you both run with the same people and live in the same town, there's not much you can do."

"So there was a romance? I wasn't sure if that was rumor or not."

"I think it was there longer than anyone knew, and one day it was over. Lydia up and left to clear her mind, and when she came back, she started buying up the town and putting her name on everything. Phillip has been there ever since just trying to get her attention. He'll never learn."

And wasn't that romantic? She up and left, and Gerald didn't follow. Well, she wouldn't have given him a moment of her time either. It wasn't even fair to compare their story to Lydia and Phillip's.

"So when are you two going to get married?" Tyson asked as they drove toward her house.

"We don't have plans yet. We haven't told anyone anything yet. We have a lot to think about."

"There are a lot of great venues in town. My sister and her mother own most of them. No matter what you choose to do, you'll have a good family on your side. And if you ever tell anyone I just said the entire Walker family is good people, I'll deny it," he promised with a wink.

"They are good people," she contemplated. "Not once have they treated me like an outcast, and they have every right to."

"Like I said—good people."

Tyson pulled up in front of Ella's house. "Get some sleep. Gerald's going to need your clear head when he gets home."

"I will. And if you and Pearl need anything…"

"We'll let you know."

After Tyson saw her inside and checked out her house before he left, Ella drew herself a warm bath with bath salts and slid in with a glass of wine.

The day had been long and unexpected. As she sipped her wine, she thought about what Lydia had endured while she and Gerald were getting drunk, fighting, and making up.

That man who had taken Lydia had destroyed lives—families. He had a vendetta against his ex-wife, and innocent women and a twelve-year-old girl paid for it. Lydia paid for it.

Tears rolled down her cheeks. Lydia's world had been rocked and shattered. And when she thought long and hard about it, wasn't it a blessing that Gerald could offer comfort to Lydia when no one else could—not even her brother.

He was a kind soul, kinder than any other human she'd ever met. He had his angry side, but didn't they all? But it was in his DNA to help when someone needed help. Any Walker would give someone the shirt right off their back.

Ella realized that she was lucky to get a second chance. Her pettiness could quickly get in her way if she didn't come to grips with the fact that Gerald loved her, and from what she'd learned, he'd always loved her.

Sinking into the warm water, she let her head fall back, and her body float. It was going to be a very long night waiting for Gerald to return.

CHAPTER 28

Night had turned into twilight, and Ella's eyes were still open in the stillness. She'd tried to go to bed and rest. She'd done everything she'd ever been taught. Warm milk. Nice warm bath. Yoga. TV. Reading. The list was significant, but sleep eluded her.

There was only one thing left to do. She thought as she swung her legs over the edge of the bed. She didn't only clean when she was mad. She did it when her mind wouldn't shut off, too.

Ella started in the kitchen, which was tidy enough since she hadn't been home to cook or eat. She scrubbed the sink, the counters, and the inside of the refrigerator. The floors were next, and then dusting and vacuuming the living room. By eight o'clock that morning, her house sparkled and smelled fresh. She opened the windows and looked out into the back yard taking in the glory of the beautiful morning. It was almost serene enough to make her forget why she'd been up all night cleaning.

Gerald, for what it was worth, had spent the night with Lydia.

Oh, her mind was so stupid to frame it like that. Lydia was in a freaking hospital with a head injury and loads of emotional and physical trauma. What did Ella expect? Gerald wasn't going to sacrifice what they had and make a play for Lydia. It was just the way the human mind worked, and who knew that better than Ella Mills, who worked with the general public and their ever-changing mindsets. She'd more than once defended someone she didn't think was innocent, but in their twisted minds they thought they were. She'd seen an innocent person change their pleas, too, because once facts were given, they didn't believe they were innocent. So she knew it was just her head playing games with her, none the less it was devastating.

And that, too, bothered her, she thought as she made herself a cup of tea. None of this should be devastating to her. She wasn't the one that had been kidnapped, beaten, and who knew what else. She wasn't dead or left for dead. And she didn't kill a man. Lydia had, and she needed her family and her friends. Gerald was a good friend.

She'd seen Tyson's saddened look when his sister turned him away for Gerald. Gerald was a friend, and sometimes people needed a friend more than a family member, especially when going through something traumatic. Ella sure as hell would rather have Candi nearby than her sister if something like this had happened to her. Not that her sister couldn't bring her comfort, but there was something about talking to your best friend that made it all seem okay. Families carried your pain and friends could help you process it.

GERALD SAT in the corner of the sterile room, his body contorted uncomfortably under the blanket the nurse had given him in the middle of the night. He stretched, yawned, and ran a hand over his unshaven face.

"You look like crap," Lydia's raspy voice broke through the silence.

"So do you, so don't go calling names," he joked as his voice found its correct pitch. "How do you feel?"

"As crappy as I look, apparently."

He sat up in the chair and wadded the blanket into a ball behind him. "Have they been in here to check on you?"

"Nearly every freaking hour," she complained. "They'll let me go later," she said, but tears filled her voice, and then he noticed them in her eyes. "Physically, I'm okay. Wounds heal. But they want to have me go to a facility for a while. You know, a mental facility."

That brought him to his feet. "You don't need that. You have family and friends to help you through this."

Lydia held up her hands to ward him and his anger off. "I do. I have a brother who would have given up his life to make sure I didn't get hurt. And that says a lot because he's a family man now. And my friends," she chuckled as she wiped away a tear. "Look at you. You slept in that chair, you drove all over Georgia looking for me, and you left the woman of your dreams to be here with me. Even Phillip..." She let out a laugh and left it at that. "My friends are invaluable. But, Gerald, I'm going to need more."

"We can get you more—more of whatever you need."

She smiled, and the tears seemed to have stopped. "I carried a lot of baggage with me before this, and I hid all of that away with my work. Now, I can add kidnapping, abuse, murder, and more to the list of things I have to overcome to become who I was—and be an even better version."

There she sat in a hospital bed, her face marred by the monster that hurt her, and she was strong enough to admit she needed help and was going to take it. Gerald only wished he was as strong as Lydia Morgan.

"So what does this all mean?" he asked as he walked to the side of her bed.

"It means that when they release me, they will take me from

here to a facility, a different hospital if you will. I'm not going to tell anyone where it is. I don't want anyone to worry about me."

"Too late. I'm already worried."

"I'm okay, Gerald. This opportunity is going to make me stronger. Tyson knows what to do about my house and bills. He's going to talk to Todd and Bethany about them running my venues. I've gone too long without dealing with things, and it's time I do. This needs to be dealt with."

He wondered if the attack from Les Martin was the only thing she was dealing with. For some reason, he felt as if there were more.

"Don't take too long to heal. Some of us are used to you being knee-deep in our business."

She laughed now and then winced when it hurt. "You need to get back to your lady."

"Fiancée," he admitted. "We're going to try this again."

"I think that's good. She never left your heart."

"No, she never did."

"And I don't think you ever left hers, no matter what happened."

He touched her hand. "I think you're right. I'd feel better staying until they come for you."

"I'm going to be okay. You can trust me on that."

Gerald leaned in and kissed her on the cheek. Yes, he knew he could trust her on that.

CHAPTER 29

Gerald sat in the car and rested his eyes for just a moment after parking in front of Ella's house. Every ounce of him was exhausted. He had texted Ella earlier to let her know he was heading home, and she'd told him to use the spare set of house keys she kept in her glove box. He felt horrible that he'd kept her car at the hospital. It wasn't the first thought on his mind when he'd sent her with Tyson.

The drive back to Macon had been long. He'd considered pulling over and sleeping on the side of the road, but in reality, he just wanted to get back. He just wanted to get some rest, but they'd have a lot to talk about.

Taking the keys from the glove box, he climbed out of the car and headed to the front door. The moment he unlocked it and walked inside, he could smell the fresh pine scent. She'd been cleaning again.

It told him everything he needed to know. Ella had been up all night fuming about him staying with Lydia. That wasn't completely unexpected. He was prepared for her to come at him with claws out. He'd get angry, and she'd feel foolish. Perhaps if he went into it with that kind of knowledge, he could defuse the situation faster.

What he wasn't prepared for was the sound of a something smashing to the tile floor in the kitchen, and the curses that followed.

Gerald hurried to the back of the house and found Ella standing over the broken coffee mug, coffee pooled at her feet, and her hands covered her face. Her shoulders bounced as she cried into her hands.

"Are you hurt?" he asked as he eased his way toward her, doing everything he could not to step in the mess between them.

"No," she sobbed. "I'm fine. I'm fine!" She dropped her hands and wiped at her mascara-stained cheeks. "I said I'm fine!"

Gerald stepped back and watched as she moved for the small closet and pulled out a broom.

"Let me get that for you," he offered, and she pulled the broom closer to her.

"I can clean up my own messes, Gerald. I can take care of myself. This is my house and my kitchen, and if I break a freaking mug on the floor, I'll clean it up."

Okay, so it was worse than he'd expected.

Stepping back, he watched as she swept up the wet ceramic mug and dumped the shards into the trash. When she ripped the paper towel off the holder and knelt to wipe up the remaining coffee, she sat down next to the puddle and cried. What else could he do but to sit down across from her and wait for her to talk.

The coffee on the floor had nearly dried before her tears had.

"I got fired," she said as she wiped away the last of her mascara. "They called me on Saturday and told me I'm not a serious enough lawyer for the firm. They landed one of the biggest cases they've ever had. They need all hands on deck, but they can't trust that I'll be good for the team. So I'm unemployed."

"Ella..."

She held up her hand to stop any further comments. "I'm mad. I'm downright pissed."

"You should be. You worked hard, and you deserve…"

"I deserve exactly what I got, Gerald." She let out a long, ragged breath. "I'm mad because I was fired, but deep down inside I'm more mad because I don't care. I didn't want to work divorce cases or fight over fender benders. I thought I did, but that's not what I'm looking for." She lifted her eyes to meet his. "I gave up something good to chase that dream, and now I don't want it."

"What do you want?"

"I want a normal life. The life I dreamed about so many years ago. The one you're offering me again."

"We'll have that, and it doesn't matter if you're a lawyer in that life or not."

She chuckled now, the tears only stains on her cheeks. "I didn't handle any of this very well," she admitted. "I got too worked up over you staying with Lydia."

"I can smell the pine," he humored, and she shook her head with a smile.

"I clean when I'm mad."

"I suppose I'll know our life is perfect when we live in a messy house."

"Now, don't go that far. Even when I'm joyous, I'm clean."

Gerald reached across the dried puddle on the floor and took her hand. "I love you. Lydia is going to get some help to manage this. She's going to a hospital where they will help her sort all of this out, and then I think she's going to take an extended trip to Hawaii. She needs her space." He licked his lips as his mouth had gone dry. "I know that losing your job doesn't compare, but if you need some time to manage it all as well, I'll let you be until you know what you want."

He'd expected her to tell him that it wasn't necessary. He

waited for her to say to him that her mad was over and she was going to be okay.

But Ella didn't say any of that. "Maybe that's what I need. A little time to process everything that has happened. I mean you have to admit, we went from not talking to engaged rather quickly."

Gerald opened his mouth and shut it again. What the hell would he have said? He'd been the one to offer her an out if she needed it, and she was taking it.

Her eyes were brighter now, and her shoulders relaxed. "I think that's what I need. I need time away to process everything. I'll make arrangements and fly out tomorrow to see my parents. Maybe for the week, maybe two. Why don't you drive me to the airport and you can stay here. It's cleaner than any hotel."

"Ella, you don't need to go anywhere. I'll take care of you—support us both until you decide what you want to do. Don't leave."

"I have to. If nothing else, I need to take the lead from Lydia and take care of me before I can take care of us."

"But we're okay, right?"

Ella tucked a strand of hair behind her ear and took a moment to think. "What happened to Lydia could have happened to me, or one of your cousins, or your sisters-in-law. It could happen again to one of our daughters." She bit down on her thumb just as she had when they'd gone to give Gerald's alibi to Phillip. "I didn't even talk to her, but seeing her walk out of that house, it's going to haunt me for a long time."

"All the more reason you should just stay here, and we can deal with it all, together."

The red had drained from her cheeks, and now she smiled at him, content in her decision. "I'm not going away forever. But I need to reconnect with my family. I find that I get so jealous over the way your family comes together and how they handle things. I need some of that. I want that."

He wanted to say he understood, but he just didn't. Her family had never been like that. Why did she think that it would be different now?

"You're part of my family," he argued.

Ella squeezed his hand gently. "I will be. You have no idea what it will mean to me to be a Walker. It's like an elite club. I realized that the other day when I happened upon their lunch. And not one of those women, Lydia included, acted as if I trespassed on their day. I belonged, Gerald."

"Then why go?"

"I have to."

CHAPTER 30

And the next day Ella was gone, just as she'd said she'd be. After they had mopped up the kitchen, she'd tucked herself away in her bedroom and made flight arrangements and talked to her mother. Gerald had offered her time to think, and she'd taken him up on it.

Now, what was he going to do?

He had full use of her car and her house, but it didn't feel right. It wasn't his home. For the first time in his life, he didn't feel as if he belonged anywhere.

The first night Ella was gone, Gerald slept in her bed, alone. When he woke, after only a few hours of sleep, he fussed over making the bed, just as she would have. He drank her coffee, ran her dishwasher, and left her house feeling unfulfilled.

Ben and Dane had texted him and said they had started in on his list of work out at the ranch. They, too, figured he needed some time to process what had happened to Lydia.

He'd heard from Phillip that she'd been transferred to another hospital, but he didn't know where. As desolate as Gerald felt, he could hear the strain in Phillip's voice telling him that he was brokenhearted.

The next call he took, as he wandered around the immaculate house in silence, was from his mother. She'd invited him out for dinner, and there was no excuse worthy enough for him to miss it.

The drive out to Walker Ranch seemed longer than it ever had. Perhaps it was that the BMW didn't rattle like his old, faithful truck. Maybe it was that he was driving slower to avoid being around people—family. Then again, it might just be that he was missing Ella desperately. She'd only been gone a few hours— but this time she promised to come back.

When Gerald made the last turn toward the main house, he could see the mass of vehicles parked in front of it. This was no cozy dinner. His mother had made sure to invite every Walker from both sides of the family. Even his uncle's car was accounted for, as was Phillip's.

Gerald parked down the road, behind Missy's car, and climbed out of the BMW. He took in the sight. Only his mother could command such a turnout on such short notice. No doubt she had pulled in Susan to help her cook.

"Everyone's inside. You can't just stand out here," Todd said as he rounded the side of the house with a garbage bag, which he threw into the can next to the garage.

Gerald walked toward him, hooking his thumbs in the loops of his jeans. "Why is she doing this?"

"Your mom?"

"Yeah."

"Walker healing. Just like after grandpa died, she brought us all together so we would remember what was most important."

"Family," he said softly, thinking about Ella's reasoning for leaving. "So what are your plans for taking over Lydia's businesses?"

Todd let out a grumble. "I always told her I'd help her out in any way, but I don't know if I can handle this. Bethany and I are going to be in over our heads."

"You'll make it work. I assume Tyson and Pearl will manage the day to day business at the *Bridal Mecca* since they own part of the building."

"Yeah, that's no worry. The other businesses all have partnerships. We have to check in on them." Todd rubbed his hand over the back of his neck. "It only comes down to managing the reception hall. How hard can that be?" He posed it as a question, but Gerald heard the statement of self-doubt.

"You're going to do fine. I'll cover your work out here on the ranch."

Todd lifted his head and looked out over the sea of cars. "Where's Ella?"

Gerald kicked the gravel at his feet. "Went to her parents' place to clear her head."

"A lot happened in the last week. Being with family grounds you. I'm sure that's what your mother is trying to do. Hell, she even has Phillip here. He's a mess, by the way."

"I talked to him. He sounded bad."

The front door opened and Bethany stood there looking out at them, her red hair piled atop her head. "You two joining us?"

Gerald slapped a hand on Todd's shoulder, and they walked toward the house. The Walkers had been through it all. Demented cops who tried to kill Eric and kidnap Bethany, ex-husbands, and ex-relatives who took the children they loved, accidents, theft, and serial killers. For a moment Gerald felt the pettiness of his sadness weigh down on him. Every person inside that grand house had been affected by something on their journey to being who they were.

As Bethany smiled at him, Gerald thought of her drug addictions and how she'd taken the time to cure herself, just as Lydia was choosing to do.

Bethany planted a kiss on his cheek as he walked through the door, and then put her arm around the shoulders of her brother as they all walked back the kitchen where his family had gathered. Brothers, parents, cousins, uncles, kids, and friends gathered for what looked like a feast. Smiles greeted him. Worried gazes caught him. Love filled him.

Ella wanted to be part of this world, he reminded himself, and she would be.

GERALD SLEPT in his old bedroom after being fed encouragement from every member of his family. He never realized how worried his mother had been knowing he was suspect in the abductions and murders of those women. She knew he wasn't involved, but she worried that someone, who thought he was, would harm him.

Family. He'd been part of that clan his entire life. He'd protected every one of those people who rallied around him, but until then, he hadn't even realized they'd rallied around him—and so had Ella.

She'd lost her job being so focused on what was happening to him. She'd gone nearly gone mad over his caring for Lydia. The past few weeks had stripped her of everything she'd worked so hard for. There had to be a way to make it up to her.

Gerald tucked his hands under his head and looked up at the shadows on the ceiling.

He knew what to do. Ella would have everything she ever wanted. He could prove to her that he was in it for the long haul and give her the family she'd always wanted to be part of.

CHAPTER 31

The old red truck had been sold to a rancher fifty miles away, and Gerald thought it had been a fair deal, even if he'd wanted more out of it. The point was, he wouldn't fear for his life in the old, reliable beast. For the first time, he had a comfy ride. Big Blue was what he would call the Ford F10 with every bell and whistle that he could get added. There were going to be a lot of miles put on that truck if he lived in town and drove to the ranch every day.

The shiny Airstream had been hauled away as well. Eric had seen to that on Gerald's request, and he'd picked out a lovely house to build there, but he'd get Ella's approval first. Even if they had two houses, he wanted her to be comfortable, but he wanted to build on his acreage. He just had to.

Gerald had met Abe for lunch and got some first-hand information on what had happened at the law firm. Though Abe had been apprehensive at first to discuss everything, Gerald found that plied with one lousy beer, the man would tell all.

From what he'd gathered, Ella wasn't the kind of lawyer that went for blood, and that was what they were looking for. She had a conscience about her that didn't always please the partners. Gerald assumed that Abe fit that same bill.

"I told her that if she left the firm, she needed to take me with her," Abe offered as he pushed up his glasses and then took a sip from his beer.

While he was in town, Gerald stopped by the reception hall to check on Todd. The atmosphere wasn't the same without Lydia's energy, and Todd looked petrified sitting behind her desk.

"She has to come back. This is not my kind of job," he admitted as he shuffled orders for beer, bread, and canned fruit. "We have a wedding here in a week. It's all laid out, but what if I mess it up?"

Gerald leaned against the doorjamb, crossing his arms over his chest, and he laughed.

"Photographer space is open huh? When did they move out?" Gerald asked.

"Last week. It was in the plans. I guess. I suppose it falls on me to find a replacement for that space."

"I'll bet Tyson and Pearl could work on that," Gerald offered, and Todd nodded.

"Right. My sister owns this building. She should be doing this and not me."

"She'll help, I'm sure," Gerald offered encouragement. "What about that little space on the end?"

"The office space?" Todd shrugged. "Tyson said he talked to Ella about it, but that's all he said."

Gerald gave that some thought. Perhaps he'd find Tyson and get some specifics.

ELLA HAD TAKEN two weeks to fill herself with family. She realized in those two weeks just how hard Glenda Walker worked to keep her children in each other's lives.

Ella had stayed at her parents' house, had arranged for her sister and family to visit, had cooked meals, and even organized an outing to the zoo for the kids. It had all been her doing, though everyone enjoyed themselves.

Part of not having a family like the Walkers fell on her too, she realized as she stood at baggage claim waiting on her suitcase.

She hadn't made herself available to her family, and they did their own thing. Glenda Walker made sure her boys were part of one another's daily life so much that it was the norm. Dinners. Lunches. She was a genius. They probably didn't even know they'd been trained.

Ella looked down at her phone to make sure the text to Gerald had gone through. She had expected to see him waiting for her, but he wasn't there. She'd get her luggage and call him outside.

Once her suitcase appeared, she moved to grab it. When she turned around, he was standing behind her, a bouquet of roses in his hand.

"They simply don't compare," he said gazing at her.

Tears stung her eyes. She'd missed him so much the past two weeks, but looking at him standing there, she knew it had been the right thing.

"These are from your mother's garden, aren't they?" she asked as she took the flowers and inhaled their fragrance.

"Best roses in all of Georgia." Gerald took her suitcase handle and laced an arm around her waist. "I've missed you," he said as they walked toward the exit.

"I missed you, too. Thank you."

"For what?"

"Giving me my space. I needed a moment to clear my mind."

"Well, I left the dishwasher full of dirty dishes for you just in case it didn't go well."

Ella laughed as she tipped her head to his shoulder as they walked.

They stopped at a brand new blue pickup truck, and Gerald put down the tailgate.

"Whose is this?"

"Mine," he said as he hoisted her bag in the back. "Couldn't drive around in the red one any longer. I've taken these two weeks to make some other changes, too."

He opened the door for her, and she climbed into the truck and admired its many features.

When Gerald climbed in, he immediately pulled her close and kissed her hard on the mouth. "We good?"

She smiled, her lips still pressed to his. "We good."

The two weeks she'd been gone, the entire town seemed to have changed. Fall was beginning to take over the colors of summer. Though it was still ungodly hot, the signs in the windows of the stores boasted back-to-school sales.

When Gerald missed the turn to her house, she glanced at him. "Did you forget where you were going?"

"No. I have something I want to show you."

He drove into the center of town and down the street toward the *Bridal Mecca*. She was surprised to find that her heart hammered in her chest at just the sight of it—the sad sight. Lydia wasn't there tending to her many businesses, and that broke Ella's heart.

Gerald pulled up in front of the bank of stores and turned off the engine. "I've been here before. What will surprise me?"

"C'mon," he teased as he climbed out of the truck and she did the same.

Taking her hand, Gerald led her to the end unit, the one she'd known to be empty, as per her conversation with Tyson on their drive home.

Gerald took a key from his breast pocket and unlocked the door.

"You have a key?" she asked, and he smiled handing it to her.

"No. You do."

Gerald stepped inside, and Ella followed. The same sweet smell of roses which he'd given her at the airport filled the space. She noticed the bouquet on a desk, and on the front of that desk was a plaque that said *Ella Mills-Walker - Attorney at Law.*

Ella pressed her fingers to her trembling lips. "What is this?"

"I took the liberty of adding a name." He mused as he picked up the plaque and looked at it before setting it back in its place.

"Okay, but what is all of this?" She scanned a look over the dark space.

"It's yours. It's your office if you'd like it. I talked to Tyson, and he'd like you to be here too. He thinks you have a lot to offer the fine business people of the town, mainly him and his sister."

Ella laughed. "My own office? Gerald, I don't know if I can do that on my own."

"You don't have to. Look on the desk."

Ella walked closer to see a piece of paper laying there. She picked it up and realized it was a resume for Abe.

"He wants to be where you are," Gerald offered. "I told him, if it all worked out, you'd be here."

Tears stung her eyes. He believed in her, he truly did. He would have believed in her all those years ago too, and she'd let herself think that by chasing her dreams it would have cost him his own. What she hadn't taken into consideration was the fact that maybe his dream was to see hers through. The sentiment was alarmingly sweet, and she swallowed those tears and took a breath.

"I don't know the first thing about owning my own business."

Gerald moved to her and took her hand. "No, but Pearl does. Lydia does. Gia does. Audrey does."

She laughed again and wrapped her arms around his neck. "I get it. I get it. I'm surrounded by good company."

He pressed a kiss to her lips. "You can do this."

"I think I can."

Taking a step back, he walked around the desk and pulled open one of the drawers. From it, he retrieved a set of blueprints which he unrolled on the top of the desk. "There's more."

"In the two weeks I was gone I played board games and went to the zoo. What did you do? Take over the world?"

He chuckled as he reached for her. "I want you to look at these."

Ella looked down at the prints. "These are a house."

"And here is the rendering."

He showed her the photos of what would be a two-story home with four bedrooms, a family room, an office, and a beautiful kitchen. The master suite alone would put any fancy hotel room to shame.

"This is your house?"

"Ours."

She lifted her eyes to meet his. "You want to build this, on your piece of land?"

"I do, but only if you'll live there with me and fill those rooms. I know it's a drive, but..."

"But multiple members of your family make that drive in or out every day. It's not that much to ask of me, Gerald. Not when you've gone through this much trouble to secure me a place of my own to work. You really believe in me?"

He lifted his hand to her cheek. "I always have."

Ella lifted herself on her toes and pressed a kiss to his lips. "Thank you."

"I have one more thing."

Ella stepped back and laughed loudly enough that it echoed through the empty space. "What more could you possibly have?"

Gerald opened another drawer on the desk and pulled out a long, black jewelry box. "I already gave you the ring, but I felt as if you needed a much better proposal than the one you got." Bending down on one knee, Gerald opened the box to reveal a beautiful diamond bracelet. "Ella, for the very last time, will you marry me?"

Tears rose in her throat as she knelt to face him. With her hands cupped around his face, and her eyes wet with joyful tears, she smiled.

"For the very last time. Yes, I will marry you."

December air swirled around Gerald's beautiful bride as the photographer took pictures of her in the frosted field near the *Bridal Mecca*. Waiting for them at Lydia's reception hall were nearly a hundred loved ones who had come from all over to see them exchange vows.

Leaned up against his pickup, in his tuxedo, Gerald watched Ella play to the camera, and he swore he only fell deeper in love with her.

"Your turn," she called to him. "Get over here."

He wasn't one to flaunt in front of a camera like she was, but he would oblige a few photos.

"You look beautiful," he said as he stood next to her. "I didn't think it was possible, but you get more beautiful every day."

"You don't have to flirt to impress me anymore, Mr. Walker. You caught me."

"Mrs. Walker, I'm going to flirt with you even when we're old and wrinkly. I don't ever want you to forget how I feel about you. How I've always felt about you."

She batted her eyes and tucked her lips between her teeth.

"Don't make me cry again. Your vows nearly ruined my makeup and Bethany had to fix me."

"All of those promises were true."

They posed as the photographer instructed them to do. His smile was genuine, and the love in his heart filled him to the brim with happiness. Finally, Ella was his wife. Their house was nearly complete. And she and Abe were building a business she could be proud of.

"Okay, I think we're done here," the photographer said. "Let's get to the party. I saw the cake. I must say you have some fine taste."

Ella laughed. "It looks like satin and pearls, doesn't it? I can't wait to taste it."

"You mean wear it?" Gerald teased.

"I swear if you shove that cake in my face, I won't talk to you again."

"Oh, yes you will. Every day for the rest of our lives."

She nudged him as they walked to his truck.

He knew by the end of the night it would be decorated with crepe paper and shoe polish. It would be a sight when he drove Ella to the hotel, where he'd reserved the bridal suite for them to start their honeymoon.

MUSIC from the hall poured out as they opened the door to their party. Ella smiled so widely that her cheeks hurt when it was announced the Mr. and Mrs. Walker had arrived. Their friends and family cheered and applauded their entrance. Immediately she zoned in on Gerald's mother wrapping her arm around her mother's shoulders and both women wiping tears from their eyes.

They shared their first dance as a married couple and drank champagne.

Reluctantly, Todd walked to the center of the dance floor to vie for the garter with the other single men, only to have it land right at his feet.

Ella's bouquet was caught by one of the young associates she used to work with, who immediately pulled Todd to the dance floor for a dance.

Gerald didn't smash the cake in her face, as she'd been afraid he would. Instead, he fed her icing from his finger. He'd never cease to amaze her.

"Hey," Todd called for them as they worked their way around the room visiting with guests. "Someone wants to talk to you," he said waving them toward the office in the corner.

As they walked in, Todd closed the door behind them. On the computer screen was Lydia.

"Oh, don't you two look like bridal Ken and Barbie," she mused, and Ella began to cry again. "Don't go crying. Bethany will have a fit if she has to fix your makeup."

That brought laughter as they sat down in the chair, Ella on Gerald's lap.

"You look terrific," he told Lydia who's eyes were bright. "I've never seen you with hair that long."

Lydia scooped her fingers through the hair that now hung just below her chin. "I hate it. When I get out of here, it's coming off."

It had been five months since Lydia had chosen to work through her ordeal by going into seclusion at a hospital. Her eyes were bright, but the scar on her cheek would remain a constant reminder. "How are you doing?"

"I'm good. I'm really good. In January mom and I are headed to Hawaii. Todd seems to have everything under control there, and he said to take as long as I need. I've done nearly as much therapy as I can possibly take in one lifetime being here, and now I'm ready for the most overdue vacation ever."

"We miss you," Ella said, and Gerald squeezed his arms around her. "We all do."

"I miss you all too. I'm sorry I missed your wedding."

"I'll save you a dance with the groom for when you get home," Ella offered.

"I'll take it. Well, you two get back to your party. When I get settled in Hawaii, I'll check back in. You both look beautiful."

"So do you," Gerald added. "So do you."

A moment later, Lydia's image was gone from the screen, and the Walkers sat alone in the office.

"She made the right choice," Ella said, looking at her husband. "She looks good."

"She does. In no time she'll be back here bossing everyone around and avoiding Phillip."

Ella laughed as she stood and pulled Gerald out of the chair. "I can hear Queen playing. We have to go dance some more."

"Whatever you wish, Mrs. Walker."

"I'm never going to get tired of hearing you call me that."

"I'll never tire of saying it."

MEET THE AUTHOR

Bestselling Author Bernadette Marie is known for building families readers want to be part of. Her series The Keller Family has graced bestseller charts since its release in 2011. Since then she has authored and published over thirty-five books. The married mother of five sons promises romances with a Happily Ever After always...and says she can write it because she lives it.

Obsessed with the art of writing and the business of publishing, chronic entrepreneur Bernadette Marie established her own publishing house, 5 Prince Publishing, in 2011 to bring her own work to market as well as offer an opportunity for fresh voices in fiction to find a home as well. Bernadette Marie is also the owner of Illumination Author Events which offers industry education as well as smaller intimate author/reader events.

When not immersed in the writing/publishing world, Bernadette Marie and her husband are shuffling their five hockey playing boys around town to practices and games as well as running their family business of carwash locations. She is a lover of a good stout craft beer and might be slightly addicted to chocolate.

We hope that you liked this release from 5 Prince Publishing.

Please enjoy the following excerpt from the next book in the Walker Family Series.

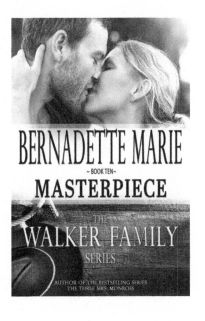

MASTERPIECE

A small heater under the desk kept Todd's feet warm as he went over the schedule for the upcoming week. He'd been thrown into the position of managing Lydia Morgan's reception hall business, and he was doing a fair job, but he missed his mornings on the Walker Ranch watching the sunrise over the acreage.

Lydia would be back soon enough, he kept repeating to himself as he answered emails, ordered provisions, and readied himself for the next bridal party that would come through the door to book their event.

In the past three months, he'd stopped stumbling over himself trying to give them every detail. He'd quickly learned, they usually knew everything about the hall, since Lydia's website was top notch. It was just customary to walk around and check it out.

His sister Bethany, who was also taking over some of the duties while Lydia was gone, would do her best to meet him and help with the walkthrough, but she had her own life with her family and a career writing books alongside her husband, who wrote the best sci-fi Todd had ever read. So he took on most of the duties, and if by chance he had time to make it out to the

Walker Ranch, he'd step in and do what he knew to do best, and that was work a cattle ranch.

But family, even family comprised of dear friends, was most important. Lydia needed to heal from whatever happened to her when she'd been kidnapped, and killed her captor. Todd was proud of her for taking full advantage of the opportunities that had been given to her to recover both physically and mentally. He couldn't even imagine what she went through.

The alarm chimed on his cell phone, and he silenced it with a swipe of his finger and picked up the file for the next bride who was to walk through the door. And like clockwork, he heard the door open to the hall.

Todd stepped out from behind the desk and walked out to the hall, which he'd set up with the lighting the bride had said she was looking for. He smiled when he heard the oooohs and ahhhs!

"Carlie Hanson?" He approached the party of six women who were taking in the room.

"I'm Carlie," the short blonde in the front of the pack said as she held out her hand to shake his.

"Todd Walker. I'll be showing you around the venue today." His eyes lifted to the women that gathered with the bride and they settled on the tallest of them, who must have been the bride's sister.

Carlie turned around to face the women. "This is my mother, Carol. My best friends Emily and April. And my maid-of-honor, my sister Jessie."

Jessie, he thought as he shook her hand and drank in the sight of her.

The other women were closer to Lydia's five-foot mark, but not Jessie. She looked Todd in the eye at six-feet.

"It's nice to meet you," he said as Jessie shook his hand.

"You too," she affirmed as she smiled at him.

Todd drew his hand back, but his eyes lingered on hers for a moment longer before he shifted his attention back to the bride.

"I've set the room up to look the way you described. I have a table up front set to your specifications as well," he offered as he led the group toward the front of the room. "We do have a DJ if you don't have one you want to bring. I've arranged catering menus for you to look at, and if you're interested, I'd be happy to take you to the other shops and introduce you around. Pearl is our resident bridal gown expert. Audrey can fit your bridal party in for hair and makeup for the big day. The florist can design all of your bouquets. And should you need legal counsel, we have that covered as well."

Carol Hanson laughed. "We've heard great things about all the businesses here. Didn't you have a photographer in the building as well?"

Todd nodded. "They moved to Kentucky a few months ago. That location has been vacant since."

All of the women turned and stared up at Jessie who let out a little laugh as she shook her head. "I'm a photographer. They think I need a studio," she admitted as she looked down at her mother who shrugged her shoulder and smiled at her daughter.

He'd seen his aunt and uncle look at their children and the wives of their children with that *I believe in you* look, just as Carol did with Jessie. His father couldn't be bothered with such sincerity, and his mother was a piece of work in her own right.

"I'd be happy to show you the space when we are done if you'd like to look at it," Todd offered.

All eyes were back on Jessie. "That would be lovely. Thank you."

Todd went back to the business at hand—wooing the bride-to-be with what the *Bridal Mecca* had to offer.

As usual, Jessie followed the women who touched every piece of silverware, looked under the tablecloths, checked the glasses for smudges, and even spun on the dance floor. This was the fourth venue they had looked at for her sister's wedding in a week, and Jessie was over it.

She loved her sister and her sister's fiancé, but why Jessie had to be involved was beside her. Shouldn't the bride and groom decide on everything? Why did the bridal party—the women—have to do it all? Jessie didn't care what flowers she had, or the color of the dresses. No matter what her sister put her in, it was going to look hideous. Her athletic build didn't lend itself to elegant dresses.

If she were candid, she'd rather be the one taking the pictures of the day and not one of the people in the background of each image. Her passion was capturing the sentiments around them, not faking a smile while immersed in the festivities.

Maybe they could have one more heart-to-heart about it. She was honored that her sister wanted her to be front and center with her, but Jessie just wasn't comfortable with it.

Now wasn't the time or place to mention it—again. Her sister seemed to be won over by the location and the women they were meeting in all of the quaint shops.

While Todd introduced Carlie to the women in the hair salon, Jessie walked down to the empty shop at the end of the building.

Cupping her hands around her eyes, she looked in.

The space would be a nice size for a studio. There was plenty of room to display photos, and it looked like there was a back room where she could stage as well.

"I have the key if you'd like to go in," Todd said, and Jessie snapped her head up to see him walking toward her.

"It's a nice location."

"Nicely priced, too."

Jessie clasped her arms behind her back, which she found she did when she was nervous, but she couldn't help herself. "Are they sold on the venue?" she asked, and Todd smiled.

"I hope so. That's my job, right? Make the venue fit the bride?"

"Is that your job?"

He chuckled as he jingled the keys in his jacket pocket. "I'm filling in for the woman who owns the building. Does it show?"

Jessie shook her head. "You did very well. What's your real job?"

"Cattle rancher."

"Walker Ranch?"

"You know it?"

Jessie tucked her hands into the pockets of her jacket and shrugged a shoulder. "I've lived in the area most of my life. You don't do that and not run into a Walker or two."

"True. But I don't recall ever seeing you before, and I'd remember."

He was looking her in the eye, and not up and down. That was a first, she thought. Men usually looked at her height and decided she was only a basketball player and nothing more. Well, they wouldn't be wrong. Basketball had paid her way through college and kept her busy on the weekends, but Todd looked into her eyes as if he knew there was more to her.

"Can I look around the space while you finish with my sister?" Jessie asked and watched as Todd pulled the keys from his pocket.

"Of course. Take all the time you want." He handed her the keys. "You can bring them back over when you're done, or I'll find you when I'm done with them." He nodded toward the salon.

"I appreciate it."

Todd turned back as Jessie's sister and her party walked out of the salon. They were huddled together giggling, including her mother. They were in their element, and Jessie was happy to be unlocking the door to what could be a fresh new start for her. She'd never owned her own business before, and the thought intrigued her immensely. She played it cool when her mother brought it up, but it tickled her inside to think about it.

If she did it, she did it on her own. No handouts. Nobody

helping her set it up or getting her business. If she was going to go into business for herself, she was going to do all the work.

As she slipped the key into the lock, she heard Todd's voice again as he spoke to her sister. Jessie lifted her head and watched as they turned the corner with the sexy, out-of-place cowboy.

Working alongside the women they had just met would have its benefits. And, if she got the chance to look at Todd Walker every day, that would be the bonus.

Made in the USA
Coppell, TX
08 July 2022